CW00520679

The Nothingman

Darren McGuinness

Published by Darren McGuinness, 2023.

This is a work of fiction. Similarities to real people, places, or events are entirely coincidental.

THE NOTHINGMAN

First edition. May 16, 2023.

ISBN: 979-8223725527

Written by Darren McGuinness.

Table of Contents

The Nothingman | Chapter 1 1

Chapter 2 5

Chapter 3 9

Chapter 4 12

Chapter 5 15

Chapter 6 20

Chapter 7 30

Chapter 8 38

Chapter 9 45

Chapter 10 57

Chapter 11 61

Chapter 12 67

Chapter 13 73

Chapter 14 79

Chapter 15 95

Chapter 16 104

Chapter 17 109

Chapter 18 124

Chapter 19 127

Chapter 20 134

Chapter 21 138

Chapter 21 149

Chapter 22 153

Chapter 22 159

Chapter 23 165

Chapter 24 170

Chapter 25 178

Chapter 25 188

Chapter 26 190

Chapter 27 194
Chapter 28 196
Chapter 29 199
Chapter 30 201
Chapter 30 212
Chapter 31 218
Chapter 32 229
Chapter 33 233
Chapter 34 245
Chapter 35 247

My first work of fiction dedicated to Jodie, my significantly better half for pushing me over the speedbumps of life!

Max, my first born who challenges me every single day to be better than I was yesterday!

Cat, for the reading, feedback and general excitement in the unsolicited....'Here what do you think of this!?' scenarios that The Nothingman presented.

Thank You!

The Nothingman

Chapter 1

It read Duke's Bar in a basic font neon, one of the letters flickered. The buzzing was tolerable, the stale smell of spilt beer and deep-fried calorie dense food hung in the air in a futile attempt to gain custom. The beer sells best here, and the food is picked at by weary, vulture like travellers on the road to their next big mistake. This isn't a place for your family meal or birthday celebrations.

He sat off to the left-hand side, in a booth that looked as if it was last cleaned when Bush was in office. The many cigarette burns reminded him of when Travis Tritt sang about the days you could smoke in a bar.

Twenty paces to the emergency exit. Sat in the corner he could not be observed from the parking lot. Thirty paces from the entrance. It was second nature to adopt the positional advantage, three men between him and the emergency exit playing pool. A half dozen 'couples' consisting of rough, unkempt men and their working girl company sat spread across as many small tables with creaking chairs like those found topping a junk heap or advertised in a thrift store as a fantastic opportunity to upcycle and add 'character' to your home. They would make an effective obstruction if he had to buy some time.

A few potential patrons came and went as he stared into his two fingers pour of a single malt he could not seem to finish. He deemed them no threat, generic, beaten-up civilians somewhere between here and there. Glengoyne 12-year-old, imported from Scotland, 500ml of the 750ml bottle sat behind the bar. He considered making an offer to take the bottle and studied the amber liquid in the glass. To the observer, he looked unremarkable, medium length dark beard, tidy hair short and dark, it was obvious he harboured a lean athletic build below his clothing, standing at 6 foot he could blend into most places and was difficult to age. Somewhere between thirty and forty. His driver's license said his name was Joel Gray, placed him at thirty-five years old from New Jersey, but that was this month.

He heard the low hum of a police cruiser pull into the parking area. One officer. Too overweight to be successful in a foot chase. He watched him operate his in-cab terminal. He sipped coffee from a thermos, used his shirt sleeve to wipe an evasive drip from his chin. The last of the coffee.

The officer exited his vehicle. Pistol holstered on the left. Left-handed. An un-even gait, his right leg given the task to take the bulk of his mass. Bullet wound or arthritis, he wondered which it was. He noticed the redness, evident on the face of the man with an increased work of breathing. Wondering whether the officer had taken his prescription beta blockers for the high blood pressure this morning.

As the officer entered the bar, he was greeted by the bartender, a subtle nod was all it took. The officer negotiated the layout of the bar with his compensatory stride even more evident. He could feel the officer's eyes study him as he passed on his way to the restroom. Looking up from his drink, he acknowledged the officer with his dark eyes. No need to speak.

He is not here for me, he decided. If he was, it would be his biggest mistake.

Despite the drywall and creaking door to the restroom, he could hear the modern digital tone from the officer's handheld radio. A traffic accident involving several vehicles on the highway was the message passed by despatch. The officer ambled out of the restroom still trying to zip his trousers at a quickened pace. A pace that was causing discomfort with his chronic pain. He wondered if he had washed his hands and made a mental note not to touch the handle the officer had used to open and close the door.

The crunching of the gravel in the car parking area overwhelmed his senses as a Greyhound bus pulled in, squeaking to a stop. A female. Approximately thirty to thirty-five years old stepped off the bus holding the small hand of a child. The child, wearing a matching backpack to the woman was fair haired and he would have guessed aged around seven years old. No threat, he assessed and noted their body language as being unfamiliar with this place.

He watched them enter the bar. Tentatively, at first, with intermittent glances back out into the world. He watched, with peaked interest. Who are you running from? The bartender acknowledged their presence by whipping his bar towel up and over his right shoulder in some rehearsed move from a 90's action movie. Small tattoo on his wrist, noted.

'Sit where you like lady.... I'll bring a menu and some water.' The bartender slurred. Not a local accent. Ex con running from his past, he assumed.

The woman led the little girl in a meandering deliberate manner to avoid any of the bar patrons. They sat in the booth next to him. The little girl stared at him and was reprimanded by a gentle tug on her jacket. He decided they were mother and daughter, similar features and he observed a subtle aura that existed between the two. It reminded him of something, somewhere, the last time he felt himself. The last time he felt happy.

Chapter 2

The Middle East, 12 weeks earlier. He sat with his feet up in the common mess room. The thick heavy desert air a constant reminder of how far from home he really was. He stared at the two faces on the laptop and could feel every second pass. Seconds became minutes and he considered those minutes. Thoughts of home. Thoughts of holding his wife and daughter again allowed him to forget the clear and present danger surrounding him.

'How old is she now?' The hulking figure of Gerald D. Hodges, squad leader asked. Grounding him from the sparse momentary escape from operational deployment.

'She is turning 6 at Christmastime'. He replied.

'Ed Truman has asked for escort back into our VIP's compound, last one buddy, then back to base for some cold ones and processing out to the real world.' Hodges continued, 'Briefing room in five.'

Fucking Ed Truman, he thought. A seriously cagey dude. CIA, black ops, and whole other bag of things to give you nightmares.

As he walked towards the briefing tent, he noted the deathly silence of the desert. The dirt crunching underfoot the only constant.

Ed Truman stood at the head of the table. Overlooking the squad. He was a stocky, mean looking son of a bitch, with amber tinted glasses and thicker longer auburn hair on the back and sides and thinned out on top. His teeth had seen too many cigars and cups of coffee.

Truman outlined the simple escort plan he had concocted that was more about making a statement than for safety reasons it seemed.

'You, Brody, lead vehicle and I want you in the rear left'. Truman ordered. 'Al-Amrit is my asset and none of you G.I Joe motherfuckers speak to him. You are the hired help. You will be compensated. You will not tell your pissant friends about this over Friday night ESPN. Uncle Sam will have you sleeping on a shit-stained mat on a black site of my choice if you so far as breathe the wrong way this evening'. Truman stormed out the tent.

Hodges offered. 'For fuck sakes. What a douche.' Standing up he continued. 'You have 15 minutes gentlemen.'

The 15 minutes were taken up by checking his rifle, sidearm and loading the Humvee. Lead vehicle. Back left seat. Quite particular he thought. Hodges sat in the right and performed radio check. Muller was driving with Andersen up top in the passenger seat.

The heavy drone of the engine that had become a source of comfort for some and brought anxiety for others made him wish he was home and could drown it out with his daughter's singing or by cranking the radio up.

'E.T.A minus fifteen minutes.' Hodges announced over the team channel.

Not even five minutes later he saw a glimmer of light through the front windshield, and then another.

Before he could formulate the words. Bang. The vehicle jolted. He felt something warm and wet spray his face as the vehicle flipped on end.

It was dark. His ears were ringing. Searing pain in his chest. Burning on his face. A heavy weight pressing him against the cold metal of the vehicle slowly suffocating him. Between lapsing episodes of consciousness, he used his hands to try free himself. He quickly realised the bulk pinning him to the vehicle was Hodges, or what remained of him.

Minutes or hours passed; he was unsure which of the two. He heard footsteps getting closer. Scratching, crunching and the moan of leather from standard issue desert boots.

He reached for his sidearm and it was gone.

'You must be one hard to kill son of a bitch Brody.' It was Truman.

Truman dragged the lifeless, maimed corpse that remained of Hodges out of the vehicle. He felt Truman's grasp lock on to his flak jacket and begin to drag him from the vehicle.

The pain was worse than he could imagine, and he drifted in and out of a literal nightmare.

He was alerted to a severe stinging on the right side of his face and tried to raise his right arm up to investigate but it wouldn't do what he wanted. Instead, it flopped by his side as he found himself sitting with his back to a large rock by the roadside. He felt stinging to his face again. He realised it was Truman.

'Fucking hold still.' Truman demanded.

'Wha.... what are you doing Truman?' Brody asked wearily.

'Well dipshit. You have at least three of your pal Hodges teeth embedded in your fucking face! I'm taking em out!'

'One of his bones, probably from the leg he doesn't currently have is currently in your right thigh. Don't worry, I've tied it off.' Truman smirked.

He must have passed out again as he heard the WHUMP... WHUMP... WHUMP... of an incoming helicopter.

Chapter 3

He lazily opened his eyes to a bright white light and the metered BEEP... BEEP... BEEP of a metronome. He assumed some sort of medical device.

An unfamiliar voice began to come closer. 'Lt Brody, good to see you. I am Dr Waller and I have been charged with your care the last few weeks. Now, I need you to understand that you have had what we would call life and limb threatening polytrauma.'

'f.. f ..f.. few weeks?' He struggled to formulate the words.

'Please, listen rather than speak Lt. there are some things you need to comprehend. Speaking will be difficult due to the sedatives and tube we had inserted into your trachea in order to keep you alive the last three weeks. The superficial wounds from the blast and subsequent objects that were embedded have been removed. Your right arm required extensive metal work to reconstruct. As did your right Femur. You developed a Pneumothorax on arrival to our unit and still have a chest drain keeping your lung from collapsing.' Dr. Waller delivered methodically and, in the manner, only a doctor could.

'Update Waller!' It was Truman. Demanding, entitled. Footsteps coming closer.

He tried to focus on the two figures in the room. The pulsing pain continued to remind him he was still alive. He craned his neck and Truman moved closer.

'Well, sir, the patient was gravely injured. He will require extensive rehabilitation and potentially further surgery. Even in best case he will never regain...' Truman cut Waller short.

Truman started clicking the syringe driver that ran a line into Brody's' IV port.

He began to feel that warm fuzzy feeling only an opiate could provide.

'Start him on the Composite Nano serum B Waller!' Truman said.

'But, sir, it has been grossly unsuccessful we haven't had time to apply...' Dr Waller protested before being slapped across the face by Truman.

That was the last thing he saw before his eyelids had had enough and he felt like he was freefalling into the black.

His understanding and comprehension of time was something he had taken for granted. He was unsure if he had been in this place for a month.... a year.... or more. His mind drifted to his daughter and his wife. Do they know that I am alive?

His thoughts interrupted by the monotone Dr

'Lt. I....' Waller was halted.

'Just call me by my name doc, I can't move my right side and there isn't a chance I'm holding a rifle again.' He grimaced as the words left his mouth.

'Well, Alex I just want to apologise for what I am about to do. They will kill my family and they mean more to me than you.' Waller said without making any eye contact.

He noticed Waller methodically attach a small bag of what looked like liquid metal or the mercury you would notice on your grandma's thermometer to the transparent tubing leading into his IV port.

As the viscous fluid slowly ran down towards the intravenous catheter, he thought this was the end. He asked himself. Why save me, why do the surgery, why waste the time if they are going to execute me?

For the first time that day or night. He could not tell which. The Doctor looked him in the eye as he spoke.

'I will sedate you for this process. You will either die or lay in stasis until it is safe enough to wake you.'

Waller moved closer with a filled syringe and pushed the liquid into the IV port.

He looked at the two liquids mix and flow into his body. Resigned to death he thought about using his only functional hand to grab the doctor and crush his trachea. He tasted something metallic. It was becoming stronger. He was acutely aware of his breathing becoming slower. The dull pulsing pain had dissipated. The bright lights in the room looked like someone was slowly turning a dimmer switch. It was dark.

Chapter 4

Muffled voices. The beeping. The metronome. Buzzing. Some sort of interference. The pain. There was no pain. His breathing, easier.

The sounds became clearer. He could feel the presence of one, No. Two people in the room. Their speech clear. Their breathing fast. The smell. A Chlorine heavy odour in the air.

He opened his eyes and turned his head in the direction of the voices. He recognised Dr Waller. The other male. Shorter. Fatter. Weasel like features studied a clipboard.

Waller was the first to notice he was awake.

'Alex, how do you feel?' He spoke. Intrigue or surprise decorated his generic face.

He sat bolt upright. Used both hands to throw the bed sheet off. He studied his hands and the purplish scarring that remained on his right arm.

'What the fuck is happening? His throat making a raspy sound in an attempted shout.

'Please remain calm. We treated your wounds. You will be home by the end of today. 12 weeks. Before you ask.' Waller coldly stated before walking out the room.

The weasel like man approached him. A studious expression on his face.

'Alex Brody, yes? I am Dr Clark and I will process your exit from the unit today. Please follow me.' He said, calculating and analysing him over the rim of small spectacles.

Alex swung his legs over the edge of the gurney. No pain. Strange, he thought. He shuffled off the edge and was shocked that his legs not only held him up but felt strong. He noticed a mirror in the room and was shocked to see a fit, healthy-looking man staring back. He wondered how on earth this was even possible.

Clark disrupted his train of thought with his nasal tone. 'You have around two minutes for questions before we reach your transport. I have limited scope in the provision of answers. Please start walking.'

He followed Clark into a long corridor. No windows. Everything clean. Everything white. Sanitary. It would take very little time to reach the end if he decided to try run.

Alex cleared his throat. 'My family, where are they? Do they know I survived? Where are we?'

Clark replied. 'Firstly, what I can answer is that you are in a specialist research and development medical facility. Location, is classified. A man of your ilk could use the term R&D site or Black site. I prefer the former. I am not permitted to provide you with any further answers to your questions Mr Brody.'

Alex, his senses peaked at the sound he was instantly aware of. An air induction unit. Helicopter. The slowing sound of Clark's generic shoes squeaked on the shiny, white floor. They were close to wherever he was being led.

Clark stopped abruptly in front of what seemed to be a positive air pressure door. He handed Alex a black hood.

'Put this on when you are through this door. If it is removed before you are instructed. You will not reach wherever you call home. I do not have authorisation to answer any further questions. Please proceed.' Clark concluded, gesturing with a hand.

Alex walked through the door and pulled the hood over his head. He heard the steps of someone wearing military boots get closer. Maybe 10 steps away he guessed.

'Hands in front. Fingers laced. I will guide you to the helicopter.' The unknown voice instructed in a southern drawl. Taking him by the hands and leading him.

Chapter 5

After the landing, standing on the asphalt, his hood was removed, and it took less than he thought to adjust to the bright autumn daylight. He could sense a presence behind him. The same unknown who had led him on to the aircraft. The air heavier, more moisture and the smell of decaying leaves filled his nostrils.

The unknown man, sporting a balaclava, walked around into his field of vision. Alex sensed no threat, the way the man moved was too hesitant, he was unsure of Alex and he knew it.

'That black SUV will take you to your home address.' The man said before signalling to the pilot in the nearby helicopter in a circular motion to start the motor. He held his gaze as he walked off toward the idling SUV.

He recognised his surroundings as R. R Jackton auxiliary airfield. Used as a military cargo annexe for the nearby Army base. He had been here many times.

As he got to within 5 paces of the vehicle, the rear left passenger door opened from the inside. Without the darkened glass he could see one balaclava clad male in the rear of the vehicle. He entered the vehicle. He smelled coffee from the man sitting to his right. Noted a thigh holster on the right-hand side. A slight nasal whistle was audible whenever he wasn't breathing from his mouth. The driver was smaller in stature. Smaller hands. Narrower shoulders. He could smell a subtle hint of a flowery product. Female he decided. Also wearing a balaclava. A lock of dark hair sat below the neckline of her chosen headwear.

It was around a twenty-minute drive to his house in midday traffic. He sat. Unbelted for the journey. He wondered why his senses seemed sharper. He analysed everything. He noticed things now that he could not have noticed before. Subtle details now seemed important to him. None of this made sense to him. He didn't know how close to death he was, but he knew he had come back from a terminus that not many men have been able to. A sudden change in his heart rate distracted him from his reflection, sit in the rear left, he remembered those words as he sat in the very same spot.

The SUV came to a halt at the kerb of number 4 Aspen Gardens. His home of the last three years. The driver exited the vehicle and opened the door and beckoned him to get out. Gesturing only with her hand. He studied the masked figure and noted that she was around 5 foot 5 inches tall. Athletic. Dark brown eyes and a whisp of dark hair where the balaclava ended, and some skin became visible at the neck. She too, was armed.

As he passed her, she maintained a distance. He sensed her anxiety in her body language. Weight distributed on her rear foot. Wide stance to lower her sense of gravity. She anticipated trouble. Was he a threat or was it the unknown that unsettled these people, he wondered. He continued to walk, and the SUV screeched away as he was on the front porch.

He noticed that there were no blinds open from the front of the house. His daughter's bike sat toppled on the grass. He smiled as he thought of Emily, how many times he had forgotten to bring it inside and the neighbour's kid was seen circling the street as he rode it, suffering the wrath of Emily when she noticed. He made a mental note to himself to cut the grass. As he approached the door. He expected the smart doorbell to activate and capture his image, the tiny light serving a warning. It was when this did not happen, he wished he was armed. The instant rush of blood, he listened for any noise, his vision sharp for any movement. He conceded that something was very wrong. His hand on the doorknob, he lifted and turned counter clockwise. He remembered there was a knack to it. The door drifted open with a squeak of the hinge. He stood in the doorway to a dimly lit living area. His sense of smell picking up dust in the air. A recent disturbance, he assessed the area. The smell of a cigar. Not burning but recently smoked, or on someone's clothing. His pulse quickened and he sensed someone watching him from the adjoining study.

Before he could act, a voice said 'Brody, don't do anything stupid. I've already saved your ass. Don't make me drop you right here and right now!' It was Truman. Hearing his voice stirred an anger in Alex.

He walked into the study where Truman stood. Now he knew where the smells originated.

'Truman, you better be able to explain this! Where the fuck are my wife and daughter?'

'Well, you'd better take a seat. I'll tell you.' Truman walked to him as he took a seat. Truman held a bottle of whisky.

'You are gonna need this kid.' Offering the bottle.

'Sarah and Emily were killed in a domestic terror attack six weeks ago. It was quick. They did not suffer.' Truman said, rehearsed, absent of any real empathy.

Alex took a breath. His chest felt like a concrete block sat on top of it, his ears begun to ring, and his throat tightened. He launched the whisky bottle at the opposite wall and flipped the wingback chair he had been sitting on. The pain he felt inside intensified, like a burning hot liquid filling every void, twisting, tearing him apart as he saw their faces in his head.

'You could have told me, in that fucking hospital! What the fuck am I supposed to do now? Who did it?' He screamed. The pain in his voice evidenced by the pitch and tone.

Truman stood over him as he crumbled to the floor and sobbed. 'Brody, they are fucking dead. You should be fucking dead. I need you to pull yourself together. I have an offer.'

'Pull myself together? I'll pull your fucking head off your shoulders! You shady piece of shit!' he shouted, getting back to his feet, enraged. He saw himself in his head, standing over Ed Truman, his face purple, eyes bulging as he squeezed the life out of him with his bare hands.

'Easy kid, I have a guy outside with a rifle pointed at your head. He won't miss. Now. Shut your fucking mouth and listen. I need you to come work for me in your miracle cured condition, you will be my asset. In return, I will give you all the information on the organisation responsible for your dead wife and little girl. Hell, I'll even arm you to bring them down.' Trumans stocky shape was outlined by the window behind him.

Truman pulled out a brown manilla file from the inside of his jacket and tossed it on the writing desk. It looked rehearsed, and something he had done before.

'Some of your questions have answers. They are in there. Others, in my head. You will get what you need after you do what I ask. Be at Jackton airfield two days from now 0900am.'

Truman walked out. Taking his stale cigar smell with him. Alex looked at the file, his thoughts flashed to Sarah, to Emily and a deal he had made with himself, in his darkest moment. He thought about his gun, how quickly he could end this by putting it against his head and pulling the trigger.

Alex opened the manilla folder. Various local news clippings made up most of the material. The most notable read:

Local woman and child killed in terror blast. Sarah (32) and Emily Brody (6) were pronounced dead at the scene of the 33rd street, car bombing. The Arc of Evermore led by cult leader Harvey Jupiter are thought to be responsible...

Amongst the clippings, was a heavily redacted CIA file on Harvey Jupiter. The information suggested that this character was the 'face' of the cult, and that the real leader was yet unknown. A starting point. Alex thought.

Chapter 6

What was left of his day, was a blur, filled with several hours of drinking whisky. Rotating thoughts and feelings, anger, depression, disbelief, and the confusion that had been ever present since the black site experience.

He woke up in Emily's bed. He could still smell her scent. Hitting him like a bat to the chest, he knew things would never be the same again. A fine layer of dust rested on every surface in the house, it reminded him of where he was comfortable, overseas, in a desert, waiting for the next order. He paced the house, his house, with one name on his mind. Harvey Jupiter. He ran a quick internet search and found out very little important information. He pulled an archive photo of the man he had never met. Never crossed. Never seen before and he knew he would kill him. Slowly. Jupiter was a forty something, blue eyed, false smiling vessel of charisma. Established himself a prominent standing in the business world. Named special guest for several charity fundraisers that he used to spread his ideology and recruit followers. Since going public with his allegiance to The Arc of Evermore, he had become untraceable. Off grid. Public listings removed. If he was to find this person of interest. He needed help.

In the garage, his jeep wrangler sat unmoved since his deployment to the middle east. He could see the vague smear of a handprint in the dust above the rear wheel arch. Another existed on the driver door handle. Truman, keeping a close eye. The obvious, a tracker and a listening device he thought. He grabbed his Leatherman multi-tool and flicked out the knife blade. Under the wheel arch he found a magnetic tracker. He stuck it to an old toolbox in the garage. In the driver side A/C vent, he found a wireless microphone and dropped it in an old paint tin.

He took a carpenters hammer and broke away a small section of drywall in the rear of the garage. Reaching in he felt the soft oiled rag that covered his untraceable firearm. It was a Glock 17, a 9mm handgun. A model composed almost entirely of plastic. Had no serial numbers and had never been used. He placed the carpenters hammer in the glove box. The gun, in the centre armrest compartment, and the Leatherman in his pocket.

He studied an address he had written down inside an old notepad and pulled out the garage onto the street.

As he drove, he observed every single vehicle and pedestrian. Wary. Alert to any possible variables or abnormalities. He drove half a dozen blocks south before doubling back and going west halfway. The journey to the address would normally take twenty-five minutes but due to the evasive technique, that time doubled.

He parked on a parallel street and vaulted a fence into a neighbouring back yard. This gave him cover and allowed him to be unsighted on approach to the rear door of 329 Abercromby street.

The wheelchair ramp that led up to the rear door was made of steel. He walked near to the edge where the frame was more likely to support his weight. To avoid alerting anyone to his presence. He could smell marijuana the closer he came to the door. Peering through the small window of the door. He could see the glow of several computer monitors.

The door opened inward and against some resistance. The piston that facilitated the automatic opening and closing for the disabled user hissed quietly under the pressure.

As he made his way into the living room, he looked down the barrel of a Remington 12-gauge shotgun. Held by a figure laying on the floor. A wheelchair parked nearby.

'I ain't smoked enough to see a deadman standing in my house!' The man said. 'Well don't just stand there help me get my crippled ass up.'

'What the hell are you doing on the floor? Alex continued. 'You are supposed to be half man half chair'

They both laughed as Alex helped the man into his wheelchair.

'I bet you got a story to tell my man.' The man said with a laugh. 'I get hit, and piss into a bag. They replace my legs with wheels. You get hit, they say you died and looky here.... You in my living room bout to ask me to do something a whole other shade of fucked up. Fuck it.... I'm game. If it pays, I'll do it with a smile.' He continued. 'Look, bout Sarah and Emily man....I.'

Alex interrupted. 'Manny I can't make any sense of it, where are they buried? Who the fuck are The Arc of Evermore?'

He passed Manny the manilla file he had rolled up inside his breast pocket. He paced the living room as Manny lit up another joint and perused the documentation in front of him.

Manny Sat in his wheelchair, deeply engrossed. The literature Alex had passed him had gotten his full attention. Muscled arms that would have rivalled Arnold Schwarzenegger in his peak. His dreadlocks reaching his lower back with veins of grey speckled throughout the black hair. Bloodshot eyes from his latest dance with Mary J. He was wearing a T shirt that read 'I skip leg day.' Alex considered it with a smile. Some of the Manny he knew flashed thought every now and then, but he was a different man since his accident.

'I checked in on em, you know.' Manny offered. 'They were told you was KIA. Something big is happening here. This fucking stinks.'

'Like we always agreed. If one of us goes down. We look after family.' Alex said. 'The funeral, what was it like?'

'There wasn't one' Manny laughed cynically. 'Fucking feds are all over it. No grounds to release. Investigation ongoing blah blah blah.'

'What can you dig up for me? I need as much on this Arc of Evermore as you can. Harvey Jupiter also.' Alex asked. 'I have to go do something. The guy, Ed Truman who gave me this wants me on a job. He is going to...'

Manny looked up from the newspaper clippings. 'You better be shitting me Brody. Ed fucking Truman? You need to stay well clear of that!'

'He pulled me out of that ambush. Took me to a Black site. Wants a favour for a favour.' Alex said as he felt a chill run down his spine. 'What do you know about him?'

Manny put down the papers and wheeled himself to the impressive arena he did his work from. A trail of smoke hanging in the air behind him. Six LED monitors made up his digital colosseum where he extracted information. His marketable skill that made him a living after having his spine severed in the middle east.

Manny typed like a man possessed. Eyes on the screen, fingers dancing across his keyboard. Images from federal databases flooded some of the screens of Ed Truman. The other screens had text. Highlighted sections spread across every page on every screen.

'This guy is bad news. CIA origins. Black ops in South America, Asia, Europe. Was moved into shadow operations after heading up a classified programme following ethical breaches and the potential risk to national security.' Manny scoffed. 'Ethical breaches and the CIA. Fucking genius statement.'

Alex cleared his throat. As he started to speak the lights dimmed and Manny's data mining setup looked to automatically lock.

'Shhhhh.' Manny whispered. 'Another visitor, front door. Get my shotgun.'

Alex stopped. He could hear slow, measured footsteps approach the front door to Manny's house. His senses erupting, feeding on the noises. He shook his head at Manny. 'No guns.' He whispered. 'He is about 10 feet from the door. Stay where you are. Pretend to keep working.'

Manny's lips stayed sealed, but his face was adorned in a clear expression. Translatable as 'What the fuck!'

Alex moved slowly into the adjoining kitchen and half closed the door. Manny sat at his desk and played along.

Through the space left by the half-closed door, Alex watched as a well-built man with a balaclava slowly entered the house. Closing the door behind him. Even over the sounds of Manny typing at the desk Alex could hear the man breathing. Heavy, with a familiar postnasal whistle. Coffee guy from the airfield, Alex thought.

The man began to edge closer to Manny's position. Alex noticed the gun holstered to the right thigh. In his hands, a thin piece of wire occasionally caught the dim light.

Approaching from behind, he wasn't more than eight feet from Manny. Alex grabbed a six-inch kitchen knife from the block. He quickly cleared himself from the door and launched the knife at the man. The blade embedded in the man's left thigh to the hilt. Before he could even let out the painful scream that followed, Alex, like a coiled spring was already close enough to launch a violent front kick that sent the man stumbling into the wall behind him.

The man screamed, he tried to address the stainless-steel blade that rested in his thigh. Reaching with both hands he hadn't felt Alex unholster his gun and rapidly remove the bolt and slide. Rendering it unusable. Alex drove his left forearm across the man's temple, and he dropped to the ground with a dull thud.

Alex used the man's own plastic handcuffs to secure his hands. Applied a battle tourniquet approximately 5cm above the wound caused by the knife and removed the balaclava. The man breathed in an almost automatic, deep rhythm as he lay on the floor in an unconscious state.

'What the fuck have you gotten into here Brody? This is some off the chain shit. Who is this motherfucker? You shoulda let me shoot him. It's been a while.' Manny laughed.

'Do you know him?' Alex asked. 'No ID, a Cell phone, and keys for a Lincoln.'

'I'm insulated brother. Anyone comes here it is family. My tracks have tracks, that have tracks, that lead to camp nowhere.' Manny shook his head. 'Generic white dude is all on you!'

Alex laid out a plastic shower curtain on the kitchen floor. He dragged the man and placed him in the middle of it and removed the man's boots and socks.

He had all but confirmed the man as the very same who had sat silent in the black SUV the day before. Blonde hair. Heavily pock marked face. Tactical gear from head to toe. He wondered where the female was.

A few minutes had passed. The man had regained consciousness. Groggy. He stared Alex in the eye and offered no words.

'Who sent you?' Alex asked.

No reply. Manny was beside the gas stove. On the stove, rested against the cast iron pot stand was the knife that had been in the man's thigh. The steel turning red from the flame.

'The SUV, yesterday, that was you. Right?' Alex stared into the man's icy blue eyes.

The man lay still. Offering no affirmation to the question.

'You will notice that I have applied a tourniquet to your leg. Don't let that fool you into thinking you will be walking out of here anytime soon. I have applied it, deliberately, may I add, to stop the circulation to the rest of the leg. I'd say twenty minutes. Give or take. Before your cells leak, muscles die, and the leg is unsavable. After that time, if you take it off, you can say hello to blood poisoning and kidney failure, hell, maybe even cardiac arrest.' Alex said with a coldness that reminded him of Dr Waller.

For the first time, the man's eyes betrayed his calm, defiant exterior.

He said. 'Truman. I work for Truman. I'm your babysitter. Until tomorrow at least.'

'Has the remit for a babysitter changed? Forgive me, I have been away for a little while. He looked at Manny and then back to the man. Have you called in? Does he know you are here? Where is the woman?' Alex stood, his face determined.

The man grinned sardonically in reply.

Alex took the knife in his hand. The bladed end glowing red.

He used one hand to hold the man's left leg against the floor and with the other, pushed the red-hot blade of the knife into the mid-sole of the man's foot. Thousands of nerve endings, reacting to the stimulus. The man writhed in pain and squealed through gritted teeth as the smell of singed flesh filled the room. His eyes watered, before he began to laugh.

'Fuck, couldn't you have made it hotter? Fucking amateur marine.' The man laughed maniacally. 'Truman asks, you do it. Sooner you understand that the better.'

Alex stood. He walked over the counter whilst he spoke. 'You clearly are not the smartest of men. I have nothing to lose. What did they do to me in that place?'

'You are Truman's future. You have more to lose than you know.' The man said with a smile. 'Now cut the shit, get these cuffs off me. I'll forget you stabbed and burned me.'

Alex turned to Manny. 'Did I ever like all that cryptic shit?'

'No, Alex, you did not.' Manny replied.

Alex quickly grabbed a plastic bag from the countertop and pulled it over the man's head. Using a roll of brown parcel tape, secured it around the man's neck in a flash.

For almost 30 seconds the man thrashed around on the floor in a futile attempt to influence the stimulus to breathe slowly being taken away. Alex popped a hole in the bag, he had made his point.

The man gasped. 'All I can tell you is that he is heavily invested in you. He needs you at that airfield. I've worked for him for ten fucking years. He's never given a fuck about a piece of shit like you! Until now!'

Alex and Manny sat in silence. They had broken him.

The man continued. 'Follow you. Babysit. Make sure you aren't compromised. Kill anyone you talk to. That's my orders.'

'Hear, that? He was gonna kill you Manny. Because we talked.' Alex tried to apply sarcastic humour but his rage bubbled over.

Alex ripped the bag fully open. Revealing the man's face again. 'What did they do to me in that place?' he asked.

The man's eyes, bloodshot from the near suffocation, blinked wildly. 'A man with nothing to lose. It's what he needs. No family. No identity. No limits.' The man delivered his speech with a punch, he knew what Alex had become.

The flash of something metallic hitting the light, caught Alex's eye. A rush of light footsteps. The back door burst open and another figure wearing a balaclava rushed in. Holding a supressed handgun.

The woman, Alex thought. She had the gun raised at Manny. Aimed at centre mass. She was going to kill him.

Alex grabbed a meat tenderising hammer from the countertop. Two quick strides, he was close enough. He struck her lead arm and a sickening crunch echoed through the kitchen. She let out a yelp and dropped the gun onto the floor. Doubled over, holding her arm. It was surely broken. Now clutching her forearm. She dropped to her knees, breathing rapidly. He could smell the floral scent she wore, it filled the room, barely masking the smell of her colleague's singed flesh.

He unmasked her and picked up the gun from the floor. She looked at him with her deep brown eyes. A slight dimple on her chin. A few locks of her brunette hair dropped to her shoulders. Her face pale but attractive. He wondered if she would have been as pale had he not broken her arm.

He checked the gun. There was a round chambered. The two would be assassins exchanged glances. Nothing said, they spoke only with their eyes. They read failure and expressed a mutual disappointment. Alex could sense their fear. Did they fear him, or Truman?

'What is your name?' He asked the woman.

'Misha.' She replied. 'I need a hospital.' Gesturing with her head. 'So does he.'

He moved towards the man and released the tourniquet from its limb strangling extreme. 'Where is your car?' Alex pulled a bag from the kitchen, placing the guns inside.

Chapter 7

The would-be assassin drove the SUV. His name was John. Misha, his colleague, sat in the rear with Alex, cradling her arm. She complained little, clearly a tough, resilient woman.

It didn't take long to get to Liberty Reach University Hospital. Alex instructed Misha to get treatment from the Emergency Department. John, with a knife wound, dressed with a basic bandage, would have to wait or seek help from an off-grid source. Knife wounds invite Police attention, neither could explain this away. Misha returned to the vehicle almost two hours later. She wore a splint that took up most of her arm and hand. A freshness in her eyes, she was not like her colleague, Alex thought. John had a darkness in him.

Alex had been given a .38 snub nosed revolver and untraceable cell phone from Manny. He had both guns, taken from his present company in the bag. Nestled at his feet. Manny was currently using his digital forensic skills on their cell phones.

'Thank you for bringing me here.' Misha said. 'I want you to know I'm just doing my job.'

John glared at her via the rear-view mirror. His darkness oozing from his piercing eyes.

She continued. 'You are not to be harmed; we need to make sure you get to that airfield tomorrow. Ed has invested in you, you know? I think you'll be leading our team; the next op is make or break for Ed.'

John shifted in his seat. Still glaring at Misha. Alex noticed the slowed breathing. The stiffened posture. He heard the two subtle clicks. A pistol's hammer being cocked.

As John swivelled in his seat, Alex grabbed Misha, Dragging her across his lap. A muffled pop. The stuffing from the seat misting up the air as the bullet passed through. Before John could fire again, Alex had already wrapped the seatbelt around his neck. A sharp pull. A sudden crack. Some rhythmical shaking in John's limbs and it was all over. He slumped as though he was a weary traveller taking a nap.

Misha lifted her head from Alex's lap. She looked from the seat where she had sat. A small plume of smoke coming from a hole where her chest would have been. She looked to the lifeless body of John and struck his head with her balled up fist. Alex grabbed her arm, and she stopped before launching another strike. She sobbed as she realised how close to death she was.

Alex broke the silence. 'We need to get rid of him. You need to tell me everything you know.'

'I'll help you bag him and put him in the trunk. Ed will deal with him tomorrow.' Misha's voice trembled. 'I thought he was my fucking friend. We have worked together for years. That was a kill shot.'

'What do you for Truman?' Alex asked as they zipped up the body bag and lifted John into the trunk.

'Mostly security, armed escort and the occasional snatch and grab.' Misha continued. 'Lately, he has had us busting labs and research sites.' She held her gaze on Alex whenever she spoke, studying, trying to read him at every opportunity. Alex wondered what she knew about him.

They drove to a motel nestled beside a recreational site. It was a few miles from the Airfield for the next day's meeting with Truman.

It read The Silent Knight Motel. Large plain text with a medieval knight, sleeping in full armour, on a bed. Genius marketing, Alex cringed. There were 16 rooms over two levels. In the lot, 4 cars and a minivan were parked up. Alex and Misha walked into the reception. A short, bespectacled man with a bald head stood staring as they approached the desk. Dolly Parton exercised her vocal cords on a small stereo behind the desk clerk.

Before Alex could, Misha spoke. 'Hey, we are passing through before deployment from Jackton in the morning. Do you have a room we could use for tonight?' A natural communicator, believable.

His name badge read Clarence. 'Oh sure, sure, we get a lotta service people here. We have a reduced rate for y'all on inspection of a valid ID.' His eyes drifting towards her breasts, not for the first time.

She reached into her bra and pulled out a driver's license that was wrapped in some cash.

Clarence smiled from ear to ear. He checked the ID and produced a key card from under the desk.

'That'll be thirty-five dollars for the night.' When he spoke, he spoke to her chest.

She handed him forty and took the key. Thanking him.

They walked back to the SUV. Misha popped the trunk and reached in next to her dead colleague. She held a backpack as she walked towards room number 3.

Inside the room, Alex checked the bathroom window. Noting its suitability for a quick exit. He checked the door for an internal chain. Flimsy. It wouldn't take much to break it. He heard the squeak of a tap from the bathroom and subsequent running water.

He was sat in a chair next to bed. Five steps to the door. Fifteen to the bathroom, unless he had to run. A few seconds to open the window. No clear view inside the room. He wondered why he now considered these things. It seemed as important as breathing to him now.

He heard the barefoot steps of Misha before she emerged from the bathroom. The water was still running.

'Alex, could you help me tie this?' She spoke with a familiarity.

She walked into the room. She was dressed only in her bra and underwear. Carrying a plastic bag.

He couldn't help noticing her body. It was well looked after. She was physically fit, and he felt something stir inside of him.

'Help me tie this over my arm, can't get it wet.' She smiled.

He did as she asked, and she returned to the shower. He left her gun by the bed, grabbed a sheet and pillow from the cupboard, and set up on the floor.

As he undressed, he was reminded of the scarring. He remembered the pain making him wish he was dead. His thigh, where Hodges bone had pierced through, smashing his own Femur. His Arm, once mangled and robbed of function. His chest, where a tube drained blood, fluid and dead tissue. His face, several small divots where his friend's teeth were lodged.

'I know you have no reason to trust me. I won't try hurt you. You can sleep in the bed.' Misha's voice interrupted his moment of reflection. She stood towelling her hair. Wearing an oversized Las Vegas Raiders t shirt. It sat around her mid-thigh. The dark shirt made her eyes look impossibly darker.

'Raiders fan?' He asked.

'Nah, just liked the shirt. Grew up around the game.' Her eyes scanning him. 'Looks like you've seen some action, the scars, I mean, ouch.'

'Yeah, three months ago, one of Truman's ops.' he replied.

'Wait, they look older than three months.' She moved closer. 'Surgical scars and trauma, that, makes no sense.' She touched his arm. Running her hand along the contours of the scars.

He recoiled, slightly, from her soft touch. 'Nothing has made sense lately Misha.' He said, looking her in the eye. 'I will get some answers, starting tomorrow.'

She leaned in and kissed him gently on the side of his face. 'Thank you for saving my life tonight.' She returned to the bed.

As he lay on the floor. His thoughts filled every second that passed. He wondered why he was scalpel sharp when considering his surroundings. People. Potential for danger or conflict. He was a mid-level operator in the marines at best. Something had changed in him. He heard things better, saw things that split second before they happened, studied every move a person made. He was better, faster, more capable of close quarters violence than he had ever thought capable. A finely balanced combination of intuition and gathering information, assessing variables.

He thought about his wife and daughter. Hoped they didn't suffer. Wondered where their bodies were. Did Emily know he loved her, did Sarah? Why him, why had Truman made him a ghost. No medical discharge from the service. No body flown home for the 21-gun salute and folded flag. He thought about Misha, she seemed genuinely invested in Truman's cause. John tried to put a bullet in her for talking about it. Nothing made sense to him. He thought about Overkill, a song written and performed by Men at Work. I can't get to sleep...the lyrics began, and finally alluded to the feelings provoked by stepping into something you cannot control.

He woke at 0700am. He felt comfortable enough to leave his gun where he had slept. Misha's supressed 9mm sat by the bed where she still slept. He showered quickly, forgetting he was not overseas and under strict water usage rule. He stood at the sink staring at his reflection as he brushed his teeth. His scars looked better than the previous day. Misha entered the bathroom without knocking, the door unresistant with the bolt missing.

'Oh shit, sorry.' Her eyes darting anywhere but his naked form. Her face flushed.

'It's fine.' He grabbed a towel to cover himself. 'I'm finished.'

He couldn't help noticing how pretty she was having just rolled out of bed. His thoughts stopped immediately with the buzz of his cell phone.

'Manny, what have you got?' He answered the call with a question.

The cell phone buzzed several times against his ear.

'I'm sending you some things as we speak. Your new babysitters cell phones were mostly cleaned. High end encryption. The dude. He had some messages I recovered. I assume they are from the Truman cat. He was supposed to ice the girl. It's mostly in code. Basically, they have had concerns over her presence of conscience.' Manny spoke excitedly. This was his area of expertise. He thrived in the information business.

'He already tried. Tried to shoot her in the car.' Alex spoke in a lowered tone. 'He's in a bag in the trunk.'

Manny started again. 'Truman is as dark as it gets. Moved outfield into free operations. Some ties with the current Vice President from their time in the Gulf. Looks like he freelances until Uncle Sam comes calling. No references to the site you were treated at. It's off grid. Just like him.'

'The Arc of Evermore?' Alex asked.

'Sent you some stuff. A few potential social sites for members. Some drop-off and pickup sites. I can't get much more on Jupiter. He fell off the map in late 2019. Some weird chatter around them and what they are up to.' Manny concluded.

'Manny, are you all in on this?' He asked. 'No matter what it takes?'

'You ain't getting rid of me now, brother.' Manny spoke with conviction.

'I'll do Truman's gig.' Alex turned to see Misha pulling on her tactical gear. 'Talk in day or two'. He ended the call.

Alex thought about telling Misha of John, and his instructions to kill her. He decided to leave it until he knew where they both stood.

He studied her getting ready. Well-fitting tactical combat trousers. Boots. A quarter zip top that hugged her athletic figure. She looked up at him as she placed her hand on her gun. He nodded in approval. She strapped it into the thigh holster and smiled. He wondered how they would explain her splinted arm.

Chapter 8

They drove to the airfield. The radio playing low, uninteresting chatter. He had re-assembled John's pistol. He wouldn't need it anymore.

'Truman doesn't need to know john tried to kill you.' Alex looked at Misha as she drove. 'I killed him before you could explain your presence.'

She looked troubled. Alex said. 'Trust me. If he needs me that much, he will accept it as collateral.'

Alex sat as Misha negotiated the track surrounding the airfield with familiarity. At the gate, she greeted the sentry, and was permitted access.

They pulled up at a large hangar. One that could have housed a Lear Jet or two. It had a Mezzanine area to the rear. The working floor, littered with heavy lockers and storage boxes. All stamped with U.S.M.C insignia. Truman could be seen having a heated conversation with a mercenary type before waving him off. The man looked like he had been released from a toy box, a plastic soldier.

They exited the vehicle, his senses stimulated with the smell, the noise and the people. They walked with purpose into the hangar.

'Upstairs. Now.' Truman demanded.

They climbed the steel steps in single file. A large table held several coffee cups, cigar ends, and a large blueprint spread across.

Truman stared at Misha. 'Where the fuck is John? What happened to your arm?'

Alex interjected. 'He is in the trunk. In a bag. Probably in the later stage of Rigor Mortis. I broke her arm, with a hammer'

Without breaking his gaze from Misha. He delivered a backhanded strike across her cheekbone. She recoiled. Eyes watering. She said nothing. Did nothing. Only stood.

Alex had to stop himself from reacting. Every fibre of his being challenged. It would reveal too much. He gritted his teeth.

Truman spat. 'You should know better! Plan better. The fuck do I retain you for? Stupid bitch!'

He could see her cheekbone turn red. He decided at that exact moment. If it comes to it. He would make Truman regret that blow.

He spoke up, before Truman decided to hurt her again. 'He came through a door too quick. I reacted. Stabbed him. Broke his neck with a belt. She came in maybe 30 seconds later. Took a hit. Identified herself as one of yours. It was too late for John.'

'Well.' Truman smirked. 'Ain't it good I only need you two for the job. Brody, it's a sort of homecoming.' He gestured at the blueprint. 'You are going back to see old Waller. You will obtain three hard drives from his data terminal. You will deactivate the Halon fire suppressant system and burn it. It needs to look accidental.'

Hesitant, Alex asked. 'We expecting resistance? What is the ex-fil plan?'

Truman lit a cigar. Leaning against the handrail he smiled. His yellowed teeth serving as a reminder to any child to make good oral hygiene choices. 'No resistance. It's my site. It has served a purpose.' He studied Alex like a predator. 'You will be taken in by chopper. You will do what I have explained. You will exfiltrate by foot. After 24 hours, I expect you to deposit my goods to the safe in room 3 of the Silent Knight Motel. It's nearby.'

Alex wondered if Truman knew they had spent the previous night there. Coincidence, he hoped.

'You leave in an hour.' Truman started walking to the staircase. Still speaking, he continued. 'Feel free to take what you want from our arsenal here.'

As Truman reached the hangar door, a blacked-out SUV arrived, and he was gone.

Alex moved closer to where Misha still stood. Aware that they could be observed, he lowered his voice. 'Hey, are you okay?'

She bowed her head, slightly, ashamed. 'I'm fine.' Her right cheek, red with some swelling. 'We've hit research sites before, but never his own.' She looked him in the eye. 'I'm worried about this. He has never hit me before. This is big.'

He nodded; they walked down the steps together. Misha opened a box and removed some black tactical clothing. 'You should get changed.' Handing it to Alex. 'Let's both at least look the part.' She smiled.

Alex geared up in the tactical clothing whilst Misha poured over the armoury, selecting her tools of the trade.

He took a Glock 17 9mm and a shortened M4 Carbine. That was enough if the op was as simple as Truman made out. Alex checked the plan, and checked again.

The start-up sound of the helicopter signalled that it was time to go as they stood on the tarmac.

They spoke very little in the air. Alex caught himself daydreaming. Thinking about a cabin in the vast green forest that sped past underneath. He hadn't had time to grieve for Sarah and Emily. They would have loved a cabin in the woods.

He snapped out of it as the bird banked right and slowed its rotors.

'Ready?' He asked Misha.

She winked, cleared the breech in her rifle, and took a deep breath. She wore an air of confidence, a comfort in herself that Alex noticed.

They cleared the wash caused by the rotors and headed towards the building in a crouched position. The helicopter was gone in seconds. Something is very wrong here, Alex thought.

'I was hooded last time I was here, never saw any of this.' Alex explained. 'You know it?'

'No, only one door though, take point, I'll cover.' She said, slowing her pace to cover the rear.

Alex quickly opened the door. A rapid threat assessment. Quiet. A holding room. He recognised the positive air pressure door that led to the inner whitewash corridor.

He cleared the door at a rapid pace. To the right, the corridor continued. Again, deathly quiet. He stayed low. Moving slowly, he reached the room he had spent the last 12 weeks laying on a gurney. It lay empty. Waller's machines sat in stasis. Waiting for their next casualty or victim, depending on perspective.

He felt Misha get closer, she whispered. 'Is that where they had you?'

He nodded and kept moving. There was a large office that provided an end to the corridor. Still in the whitewashed, sanitary style theme. They entered the room. Alex peeled off to the left and Misha went right. A quick assessment. No threat. Alex pulled three heavy duty hard drives from a freestanding unit and in the same motion, placed them into a bag.

Misha let out a gasp as she stood behind a workstation. 'Alex, you better come over here.' Her cool exterior, compromised with what she had saw.

Alex stood at the opposite side of the desk. Looking at the floor, he saw Dr Waller, motionless. His Achilles tendon, severed on both ankles, had stopped bleeding. Face down, a small pool of dark, almost black blood gathered around his head, thick, congealed.

Misha leaned down. Placing a hand on his lab coat, she tried to roll him. She instantly recoiled as he let out a wet, crackled gasp.

Alex rolled him in one sharp tug. Dr Waller lay on his back. Mouth wide open. They had taken his tongue.

Dr Waller's eyes locked on to Alex. Some relief in his eyes. He gargled his own clotting blood. They dragged him to the nearest wall and propped him up. His breathing laboured, he spat a mixture of blood, clots, and tissue onto the ivory white floor.

'Are you the only person here?' Alex asked.

Dr Waller nodded. He waved a hand at the workstation. It was then Alex noticed his hands. They were grossly deformed. Smashed up with a heavy object.

Misha asked the Doctor. 'What do you want? The pen?'

He shook his head.

She pointed at various tabletop items until he nodded.

'Coffee thermos?' She asked.

He nodded and gestured for her to throw it onto the ground. The mangled fingers flapping in the air.

She looked at Alex. He gestured, not knowing why, for her to smash it.

The thermos smashed into several pieces of ceramic on the floor. A silver, bullet like pen drive lay on the floor amongst the debris.

Alex picked it up, looked at the mess sitting on floor that was Dr Waller. 'What is this? Insurance?' He asked. 'Does Truman know about this?'

The pale, deathly looking man shook his head. His eyes filled with tears until they ran down his cheek. Mixing with the blood and gore around his mouth.

Alex noticed a change in Misha's breathing, she was trying to detach, emotionally withdraw from what presented at her feet. A man in the throes of pain, closer to death than life, unable to speak, walk, or use his hands. He was an island. Isolated. Crying.

Her eyes, betraying her tactical special ops appearance, filled as she looked away.

'Doc, we can get you out of here.' Alex offered.

Resigned to his fate. The Doctor shook his head, sobbing. He gestured with his mangled hand across his throat. Alex knew what he meant.

'Hey.' He spoke to Misha. 'Can you go disable the fire suppression system?'

'Yeah.' She spoke in a raspy voice before clearing her throat, quickly leaving the room.

He waited until she was halfway along the corridor. Crack. He shot Dr Waller through the head. The wall behind him decorated with the inside of his head.

He stabbed holes in several bottles of cleaning fluid and medical grade alcohol. Kicked them around the room and corridor. Spilling their contents. He cut a length of fabric from a jacket that sat over Waller's chair. Stuffed it into a bottle of alcohol that he placed on Waller's lap. He flicked Waller's engraved lighter he found on the desk. The flame danced as he held it to the fabric.

He almost collided with Misha as she rushed through the external door. 'Let's go, it's done.' Alex said calmly. 'Head toward the fence, we can use the forest as cover.'

Chapter 9

After walking through the forest for almost two hours, they stopped for some rest. They sat on a felled tree and took the opportunity to take aboard some fluids.

Misha was first to speak. 'I think I am finished.' Staring at her boots, she continued. 'I thought I'd get out before Ed put me on something like this. This is endgame type stuff. Soon as we hand that over. I'm dead.'

'I think you are right, Misha.' Alex said. 'Whatever is on those drives could burn Truman. He has ties to the very top. Oval office ties.'

She looked at him, fear in her eyes. 'What are we going to do?'

Alex stood up. 'I'll give him what he wants. If you want to break off now. I'll say I killed you for trying to take the drives. Do you have cash? Somewhere to lay low?'

'Alex, stop.' She interjected. 'It stinks, something is wrong but I must see this through. You saved my life. I won't bail on you now.'

He put his hand out to help her to her feet. 'You owe me nothing.' They stood looking each other in the eye. Alex could feel the tension between them and broke eye contact first. He turned to start walking. She still held his hand, stopping him from starting down the hill.

'I'm all in.' She smiled.

Alex could hear tyres against gravel. Using the GPS on his phone, he had navigated them to a resting place for weary drivers at the side of the road.

They reached the clearing where a Ford F150 sat idling. The driver's feet poking out the driver side window. They had already stripped their rifles and stuffed them into the bag. Their sidearms, stuffed into waistbands, concealed by their clothing.

The driver almost jumped out his skin when she approached the driver side door.

'Hi, sir, me and my husband here are kinda lost.'

The man made no effort to hide his lustful stare as he studied her where she stood.

'Where y'all supposed to be?' He looked at Alex, and back to Misha. 'Y'all are a bit aways from anything out here.'

She fluttered her eyelashes, smiled, and replied. 'Well, we went a trek up and through, followed the river, and got lost. Our car is at the something Knight Motel.'

The man snorted. 'Hah, fuckin silent Knight Motel, got myself the clap last time I stayed there. Didn't piss straight for a month!'

Misha acted shy in response to his profanity.

'Sorry ma'am, sir, hop on in. I'll take you down.' His face reddened.

They reached the Motel around forty minutes later. The man's conversation was less than riveting. He veered into the rumble strips on several occasions. Taking his eyes off the road and fixing them on Misha's breasts. Alex wished they had walked the whole way.

The same vehicles sat in the lot. Clarence sat behind the check in desk. Same clothes. Sweat stains at his underarms. His odour had upped a level since the previous night. He peered over his glasses as they stood in the foyer. A long stray nose hair tempted Alex to reach out and yank it out.

Misha spoke first. 'Room 3, It's reserved for us.'

'Yes, yes, of course, your friend was here earlier. Rooms paid for three nights. We can do linen changes every morning for an extra..' Clarence was stopped by Alex taking the key from his hand.

'Bill us for extras on check out, Clarence, it's been a long day.' Alex shut down the conversation and walked out. Misha winked at Clarence, and he began to sweat almost instantly. His wildest fantasies probably playing out in his head.

Alex unlocked the room and systematically assessed the risk, this action a second nature, everywhere he went. He gestured to Misha, she entered with their bags. She kicked off her boots and threw herself on to the bed.

Alex located the safe and placed the three hard drives inside. He set a code and it locked. He stepped up onto the bed and reached up to the smoke detector. Misha, startled, had a look of confusion on her face. He unclicked the carcass of the device and ripped a pinhole camera out of the circuit board. He shook his head and walked over to the only artwork that hung in the room. He removed it from its mounting, flipped it and pulled another camera from a recess in the frame. He lifted the cordless phone from its cradle and smashed it against the bedside table. A tiny listening device, stuck to the speaker hung loose. He flushed the items down the toilet and returned to the room.

Misha's face gave him an idea of what she was about to say. 'What the fuck?' She whispered.

'I want to think it was Clarence, hoping to have a nice evening watching you undress.' He laughed. 'This is Truman. A reminder. He's seen me putting the drives away. That'll keep him happy.' He pulled his civilian clothing from the bag and began to remove the tactical gear he wore.

Misha stripped off and put on a pair of tight black jeans, a fitted Led Zeppelin t-shirt and sat on the edge of the bed. She alternated glances between Alex as he changed and a cell phone, he had thrown her.

'Do you know any of the places listed there?' He asked.

'Two places, yeah, the farm is between here and town. Duke's is a couple of miles before the state border.' She thought about the third location. 'I think that's a warehouse, can't be certain though. What are they?'

'Places of interest. Where I can get access to The Arc of Evermore.' A determined expression on his face.

'What do you want with those whackos?' She placed the cell phone on the bed and walked to the mirror, inspecting the damage left by Truman.

'They killed Sarah and Emily.' A look of determination set in. 'They are going to wish they never existed by the time I am through.'

'I'm sorry.' She offered. 'I wanted to ask, but I didn't want you thinking I was digging for information.'

'This is Manny's work, getting these locations.' He watched her wince as she touched her cheek. 'Truman says he has more for me. Part of his payment for today's work.' He walked into the bathroom and returned with a cold, wet, cloth. He placed it gently on her cheek. Their eyes met and he quickly broke eye contact.

'I need to call Manny.' He walked to the bed and picked up his cell.

'Yo.' Manny answered.

'Hey, I have something for you. The less said on the phone, the better.' Alex said. 'Need your skills. A.S.A.P.'

'Course my man.' Manny, his interest peaked. 'When will you be here?'

'Tomorrow, been a heavy day, need to be sure I am not drawing any heat to you again.' Alex said apologetically. 'Tomorrow.' He hung up.

Alex turned to Misha. 'Hungry?' He held up car keys he found in the safe earlier.

'Absolutely.' She beamed. 'Where did those come from? Are we going in style?'

They locked up the room. Misha had to be persuaded to leave her gun in the room. Alex carried only a knife. He decided they would avoid trouble. Taking a moment off the clock.

It was several miles to the nearest diner. A typical 50's style diner. Burgers and shakes. There was an adjoining bar named Betty's. He wished he hadn't noticed but details seemed to be instinctual these days.

Alex requested a booth near the back. A good view of the entrance. A waitress brought some water and two menus. She looked tired. Chewed gum and smoked too much. Her lips lined by gripping the cigarettes, aging her beyond her years.

Alex ordered a burger with fries. To his surprise, Misha did too. They ate in a comfortable silence. Interrupted only by the waitress, checking their satisfaction. They made small talk as they waited for the cheque.

Alex felt his cell buzz in his pocket. He excused himself to the bathroom. He felt the onset of a headache, his ears began to ring. He pushed a stall door open. The headache, a sharp burning to the temple. The ringing, drowning out all other noise. Beads of cold sweat accumulated at the nape of his neck. He felt a weakness in is legs and eased himself down the wall. He sat with his head in his hands. Shaking. A few moments passed.

He managed to get himself up and doused his face in cold water. The mirror betrayed how he had just felt, casting back the face of a well man. He asked himself what the hell had just happened. He checked his messages. Manny wrote:

AB. Your man. John. Had 10 Gs in his checking account. I've sent you half to the instant pay account on the cell. M.

He left the men's room. Composed. He decided not to tell Misha what had happened. The waitress stood, engaged in conversation with her. Misha had paid the bill. She subconsciously scratched at the skin under her splint. Cash grasped in the waitress's hand; she waved her off heading to the server's base. They exchanged a glance as he approached, and Misha took Alex by the hand.

'Let's go next door, I could use a drink.' Misha led him towards the door.

They entered the bar. Country music played. A bear like bartender stood chatting to a few girls sat at the bar. A couple of rednecks hovered over a pool table. An older couple played cards at a booth; a pitcher of beer sat between them.

Alex grabbed a tall table with two stools. Misha went straight for the ladies. She passed the rednecks, and they made no effort to conceal their predatory stares. Her tight jeans giving them something new to drool over as they passed comment between the three.

Alex decided. If they touched her or harassed her when she walked back. He would hurt them. He felt something towards her. For her. It felt wrong that he hadn't said goodbye to Sarah and here he was. His pulse quickening when he looked her in the eye, he was prepared to kill for her. He remembered how he felt when Truman struck her.

Misha walked out of the ladies. She tucked a lock of hair behind her ear and kept her eyes on Alex. The rednecks did nothing but stare as she passed. Alex stood; they met in the middle of the bar. He ordered a light beer; she ordered a Jack Daniels on the rocks.

For a few hours, they both forgot the events of the day. They laughed and had a few more drinks.

'Ever married?' He asked her. 'Sorry if that's too personal.'

'No, it's not, and no, was waiting for you.' She said, flirting, giggling. 'That the answer you wanted?' She studied his reaction.

'I have more baggage than a commercial 747.' He joked. 'Besides I broke your arm. I anticipate your revenge.'

She placed her hand on top of his. 'There is something different about you. I've worked with a lotta guys. You see things, hear things, it's abnormal. In the nicest way. The speed you move at.' She furrowed her brow. 'I haven't seen anyone come out better up against John. You stopped him killing me. Snapped his neck like it was a celery stick.'

She ordered another round from the bear man.

The rednecks had moved closer. Sitting at the bar, Alex could hear them hypothetically discuss Misha. What they would do to her. How much they thought he was he paying her by the hour. It angered him and he was glad she was unaware as she bobbed her head and sang along to Tricia Yearwood's she's in love with the boy. Slightly out of tune. A few words mixed up, but the foundations were there.

Alex leaned in. 'Let's finish up and head back.'

She nodded and tossed back her JD in a single action. 'You might need to drive. I'm a walking talking DUI.' She winked at him before bursting into a giggle.

As they walked toward the car, Alex noticed a pickup with a company logo on the driver's door. Rudy's Quality Construction it read. The very same as the redneck trio in the bar had written on their shirts. He stopped walking. He pulled out the combat knife.

'Gimme a sec.' He said to Misha.

He stabbed a hole in each tyre. Reached up into the arch and severed a brake line. The fluid leaking into the gravel of the parking lot.

Misha smiled. 'Aww look at you, sticking up for me.'

Before he could reply she added. 'I heard some of it.'

He could feel his face flush in the cold air as they walked to the car. He had drunk more than he intended. He worried about the effects of alcohol and the effect on his perception, his edge.

They arrived back at the Motel. He noticed no changes from earlier. It was dark. Clarence sat at the desk. He parked the car in the spot he found it. They entered the room and locked the door. He sensed no changes. Nothing in the air. Their items exactly as they were left.

Misha sat on the bed. 'Those guys at the bar. You had a look in your eyes'

'Yes.' Alex said. Placing his gun within reach of where he sat. 'I don't want any harm coming to you. They were a few more drinks away from laying hands on you. It's unacceptable.'

'Thanks for looking out for me, I'd have fucked them up though.' She said before removing her Led Zeppelin t-shirt and jeans. 'I need to wash some of today off me.'

He watched her, admiring her body as she disappeared into the bathroom and started up the shower. He rolled out a sheet on the floor. Checked his cell phone for any further messages from Manny. None.

He must have drifted off for a few minutes before he was awoken by her speaking to him. 'You are breaking my heart laying on that floor.' She stood, wrapped in a towel. 'Please, come sleep in the bed.'

He didn't protest and climbed into the bed. He couldn't help but watch as she slipped her oversized t-shirt over the towel. Pulling down to her mid-thigh before kicking off the towel. She climbed in next to him. He could feel her warmth close to him. He smelled the floral body wash she used.

He was first to speak. 'Misha, thanks for tonight, for a moment I was able to forget the shit show that has become my life.' He was still caught off guard at her directness, her projected loyalty.

She looked him in the eye. The attraction between the two was palpable. She leaned in and they shared a kiss for a few moments. 'I enjoyed myself too, you sure are something Alex Brody.' She smiled, rolled over, and turned out the light.

The next day, he already showered and was sitting with his first instant coffee of the day as Misha woke.

'There's a coffee by the bed.' He said. 'It ain't good but it ain't as bad some I have had the displeasure of drinking.'

She thanked him, sitting up, he could see Trumans mark still present on her face. It stirred up some anger inside of him. He rolled Waller's pen drive between thumb and forefinger. Slight concern washing over him for what could be on it.

Misha was dressing as the sound of parking lot gravel crunched under the pressure of a vehicle. Alex reacted by checking his Glock was good to go. He positioned himself at the window by the door and peered through a gap in the curtains.

'It's Truman.' He said. 'Three guys, one staying with the car.'

Misha removed the suppressor from her gun and concealed it in her waistband.

Alex continued. 'Truman looks unarmed, the other two, shoulder holsters under their jackets.'

A slow, exaggerated knock. Three times. Alex planted a foot close to the arc the door would follow. If they rushed the door, it would bounce back, buying a second for him to start shooting.

He opened the door. About a quarter way.

'Brody.' Truman said with a smile. 'I know you have what I asked for.'

Truman and one goon entered the room. The other stood on the other side of the door. He carried a black sports bag. Looked weighted.

'In the safe.' Alex said.

'I know, get them out.' Truman said whilst he glared at Misha.

Alex unlocked the safe and removed the three heavy duty hard drives. He placed them on the bed that separated Truman and Misha. He stood in front of her, blocking Truman's view.

Truman looked at them on bed and stood silent for no more than 10 seconds. Another tactic. Alex had seen it before, an effort to force a break in the silence. It identifies a weak link, reveals who has something to hide. No one spoke. He sensed the fear in Misha.

Truman emptied the bag's contents on to the bed where his latest acquisitions lay. At least ten rolled up bundles of cash. A cell phone. A brown envelope.

'Twenty grand. Your pay for the work, Brody. More intel on The Arc.' Truman said as he jutted his chin toward the items.

His goon gathered the three hard drives and placed them into the bag, handing it to Truman.

'Misha, let's go, you have run your race.' Truman turned to walk out the room. 'Your severance package is back at Jackton.'

'Not gonna happen Truman.' Alex said.

Truman stopped. Turned slowly to face them both. A false smile adorned his face.

'Ass like that. Them tits. Your dead wife ain't even in the ground and you are fucking...' Truman didn't get to complete his sentence.

Alex had him pinned against the door with the point of his blade pressed against his trachea. His Glock, pointed in the face of Truman's goon.

Truman raised his arms. Pushed his amber tinted glasses farther up his nose and spoke. 'Okay, okay, too soon.' His yellowed teeth emerging as he smiled, uncomfortably.

Alex stepped back. Re-sheathed the knife and tossed the gun on the bed.

Trumans goon postured and looked for the nod to attack Alex. Tuman smiled, 'Diego, he will kill you before you get your gun out or step toward him. This one is special.' Truman dabbed his neck with the back of his hand, checking for blood. 'I'm sorry. Lemme make a call. I can make some peace between us but, she, is your problem. I don't pay her. I don't trust her. You pay her outta your cut.' He held focus on Misha as she stood in the same place before making a call on his cell.

Alex looked at Misha. She breathed easier. He winked at her as soon as she made eye contact.

'Arthur. It's Ed, remember that little thing I helped you with? Well, the time has come to pay the piper. Be at your office in an hour.' Tuman ended the call. 'Brody, leave your shooter, the blade, and her here. I owe you for my lack of decorum.'

Alex nodded to Misha to reassure her. He followed Truman out to the car. Truman passed instructions to his team who crossed the lot and got into a waiting car.

Truman drove the SUV as Alex sat in the passenger seat.,

Chapter 10

The car pulled into the lot at Liberty Reach Hospital. Truman parked up next to a Crown Vic. It was tagged with tax exempt plates. Alex thought government or law enforcement, maybe federal. They walked into the building and took a lift to the lower depths of the building. A short, fat man stood in anticipation as the doors opened. A head of salt and pepper hair and a Tom Selleck like moustache.

The man spoke. 'Good to hear from you Ed.' He cast his eyes over Alex. 'One of yours?' He asked, concerned look on his face.

Tuman nodded. 'One of mine. I need you to show him the things from the 33rd street attack.'

Alex instantly understood where they were headed. The smell of Formaldehyde, the stainless-steel gurneys lining the corridor overwhelmed his senses. A cold sweat set in as they walked towards an office.

The man punched in a code. Deliberately blocking Alex's view of the keypad at the door.

Two autopsy reports sat on a table. Alex couldn't help thinking the man knew why they were coming. Had Truman set this in motion. A card up his sleeve. Something he could invoke to keep Alex in check. Questions filled his head.

The man spoke to Alex. 'Sarah Brody, Emily Brody, both victims of an attack by the T.A.E. Cause of death, catastrophic organ damage and internal haemorrhage. Blast trauma. Suggestive of moderate proximity to an explosive device. Severe burns to both, caused by proximity to an ignition source post-mortem. Carvings of the letters T , A, and E inflicted by a bladed object. Also, post-mortem.'

Alex trembled, he felt his heart pounding, every breath fighting to get out as his throat dried up and tightened.

The man walked over the stainless-steel wall that held a dozen small doors. Sparing no consideration for Alex, he opened two doors and pulled out the slabs. As he unzipped the bags, Truman stepped back, his eyes fixed on the floor.

Alex looked at Emily first. She was too small to be in a place like this. She hadn't lived enough to die. His eyes filled with tears. She was faceless. The trauma, the burns, the inscription gouged into her scorched flesh rendered her unrecognisable. He let out a haunting scream and struck the neighbouring door with a fist. A noise that would be heard down the corridor. He felt sick.

Blood dripped from his hand on to the floor. He stood looking at Sarah. She too, was grossly unrecognisable. No distinguishable features were visible. She had a tattoo on her right wrist. If it was there, the burned flesh concealed it, he saw nothing.

The man stood looking at Truman. A look of shock across his face. The colour had drained from his once red cheeks. He mouthed the word 'Husband' to Truman, and he confirmed with a subtle nod.

The man offered his condolences to Alex and explained a federal ruling that prevented them being buried. Alex heard none of it, but he was aware the man had spoken.

As they drove back to the Motel it was Truman who spoke first. 'There is intel on the bastards who did it in the envelope in your room. Some locations you should visit. If you need weapons, vehicles, anything. Take whatever from the hangar at Jackton.'

Alex sat in silence until Truman spoke again. 'The cell phone, only my number stored on it. Direct line to me. When I have more work. I'll call.'

Alex got out the car and walked towards the room. He saw Misha using the space between curtains to assess the danger. As he closed the door to the room, she hugged him. She studied his face and asked. 'Are you okay? I was worried you weren't coming back.'

He looked into her eyes and traced a finger down her cheek, following her jawline, down to her chin.

'He took me to them. Sarah and Emily. I couldn't even recognise them. They. They were a mess.' He said, clearing his throat, suppressing his emotions.

'Ohh, Alex, I. I am so sorry.' Misha said, her voice wavering. 'I can't even imagine.'

'I need to get that pen-drive to Manny.' He changed the subject, fearing he would lose it.

He was stopped in the middle of gathering his things by Misha. She held his hand where he dented the steel in the morgue. 'What happened, I never saw that today?'

'Happened an hour ago. I hit a door.' Alex said as he studied his knuckles. He wondered why the lacerations and bruising looked as though it had already been there a day or two.

Misha decided to change the subject. She didn't want him to remember the horrors he had seen not long ago. 'Are we going to see Manny tonight?'

'Yeah, take everything.' Alex said. Throwing the cash, cell phone and envelope in his bag.'

They loaded the car. Checked it for trackers and other devices and headed for Manny's. His mind raced, he thought of the ways he would hurt the people responsible, deciding to change the subject. 'You got family?' He asked.

'Military brat.' She laughed. 'Parents are both dead. Mom, cancer. Dad, cancer by proxy I guess, drank himself to death after the passed. Born in Germany on base. Grew up in LA.'

'How'd you end up working for Truman?' He said.

'He recruited me from the private sector. I worked close protection for a few Israeli diplomats. Got some joint training with Mossad. Had a decent name for myself.' She recalled in light reflection.

'I'm going after The Arc of Evermore. I don't expect you to hang around. You can take the cash; I can get Manny to transfer you more. I hear Cuba is nice this time of year.' Alex said, hoping she would sense the sincerity in it.

'I know you are trying to protect me, maybe you don't trust me. I'm here because of you. I'm here because I want to be.' She reached over and touched the nape of his neck as she spoke.

He didn't want her to leave. He hoped she would stick around.

Chapter 11

In the street behind Manny's, his Jeep still sat unmolested. They transferred their bags to his car. Leaving the weapons Truman had provided in the trunk of the car he had also provided. His Glock, where he left it. The hammer, in the glovebox.

He boosted Misha over the fence at the rear of the property before scaling it himself. They used the back door to enter Manny's place, he was in his usual spot in front of his digital playground.

'My man!' He shouted. A spliff hanging from his lip. 'Lady. Good to see you again.'

Misha smiled. 'About last time, I'm sorry.'

Manny looked at Alex and then back to Misha. 'How's the arm?'

'Ah, you know, painful.' She giggled.

Manny sat nodding to himself as he considered her, before laughing. 'She's alright by me.'

Alex felt a headache coming on and tried to excuse himself. He held his hand to his temple and the ringing in his ears drowned out everything else. He made it only a few steps before he eased himself to floor, sliding down the wall.

Misha rushed to him. She spoke but he could not hear her, only saw her lips moving. Manny became animated and wheeled himself closer. Alex held his eyes closed tight, until the pain stopped and the ringing subsided.

When he opened his eyes. He started up at Misha. His head rested on her lap. The cold from Manny's floor on his back. Misha said. 'Hey, don't move, are you alright?'

He cleared his throat. 'Yeah, just a migraine. I'm tired, they are worse when I'm tired.' Inside, he worried. He had no explanation. This was the second time. He decided he would tell Misha another time.

They had a few beers as Manny told Misha stories of the days spent training for the U.S.M.C. Laughs and smiles consumed the next hour or so. He made light of the fact he was wheelchair bound before recounting the story.

He acted it out, jokingly blamed Alex and showed of the scars from the shrapnel, and the three separate surgeries performed to help him walk again. He never did.

They looked like everyday people, socialising, sharing beers, and living in that specific moment in time.

Manny decided to break off and present some of his findings.

'Couple things have come up, some bad and some good, but a whole lotta bad for the fuckers that did the thing. You don't exist. No military history. The attack in the sandbox, didn't happen. No grave site. No social security numbers.'

Alex let out a subtle laugh. 'Did they delete my Facebook?'

Manny continued. 'This is only possible when it comes from the top. By top I mean, a man in a chair so high he has fucking sherpas scaling his crown. Like, snow falls 365 days man.'

'So what's the bad news?' Alex asked with a smile.

Misha stirred in her chair. 'Why would they do that to someone. I knew Ed Truman was another level of player but not to this scale.'

Manny took a sip of a beer and lit up a joint. 'He goes back to the Gulf with the VP, President in waiting man. He must be involved. That magic marker ain't available to just anyone.' His smoke hung in the air. 'I have gotten you a couple of other identities. Dead folk. Grade A counterfeit ID's. Not the ones we used in High School.' He laughed and pulled a half dozen Driving Licenses and Passports from a drawer. Alex took them.

'Joel Gray.' Alex laughed

'The Gray man.' Alex and Manny said in sync, laughing.

Manny continued. 'So, anyone you grab from The Arc of Evermore.' He pulled out a small cigarette packet sized box with a cable and port connector. 'Use this to clone their cell. I can find out who they talk to. Where they've been. Where they live. What porno's they watch. Empty their bank account. You name it. I'll do it.' He paused. 'That's how we get Harvey Jupiter.'

Alex excused himself and headed to the bathroom.

Manny spoke to Misha. 'You along for the ride or you got a stop coming up soon?'

'I'll do anything he asks of me.' She shook her head. 'The things he has been through. I. I don't know how he's still going. I think I'd be dead twice over if it hadn't been for him.' She looked at her boots, reflecting on the last few days.

'You and me both. He's different. I don't mean different with the Sarah and Emily thing.' He offered her a pass of the joint and she shook her head. 'The way he moves. The way he thinks. It's changed. The way he took out your buddy. That shit can't be taught.' Manny wore a confused expression on his face, as he studied his spliff, as though it held the answers to the secrets of the world.

'I've never seen someone disobey Ed Truman and live. But Alex. He pinned him against a wall with a knife to this throat. Get this. Truman apologised. I don't know whether he needs him. Fears him, or both.' Misha said.

'Why the fuck he do that?' Manny asked letting out a plume of smoke.

'He had to understand that Misha is off limits.' Alex said. 'Playing the dead wife card made it more important to let him know he can be gotten to.'

Misha felt her face flush a little. Manny wondered how much he had heard of their conversation.

'I know I'll never be the same again. I've lost part of me that I can never replace. I can't replace what I've lost even if I kill every single piece of shit associated with this Arc of Evermore. I will make sure they can't do this to someone else. That I promise.' He continued. 'Truman and Waller did something to me. I feel, awakened, sharper, I process risk every single second. I'm planning exfiltration for every possible outcome.' Alex stopped, noticing Misha begin to tear up. 'I want you with me, but only if you want to and don't feel that you owe me or need to go along.'

She stood and made her way to the bathroom. He heard her sniffling and decided to give her some space to compose herself.

Manny broke the silence. 'Dude, she is all in. She is like us man. She owns her shit, don't need protecting either.'

Alex ran his fingers through his beard as he realised the scale and potential of what Misha had to absorb the last few days.

'I wish a chick looked at me like she does you AB. I'd understand if you hit her in the head with my tenderiser. That would make sense. Mush for brains.' Manny laughed.

Alex brushed the suggestive statement off. 'On Truman's gig. It was the facility I was treated at. The doc was maimed. Tongue cut out. Hands crushed. Tendons snipped and unable to walk.'

'Sounds like someone tying up loose ends.' Manny sat shaking his head.

'He was still alive. He begged me to end it.' Alex sipped his beer. 'I shot him and followed my orders. Burned the place to the ground. Strange thing is, no news coverage. Upstate research site sharing a boundary with a national park area, that gets a slot on the evening news but, nothing.'

He tossed the pen-drive to Manny. 'Gave me this before he asked for a bullet.'

Manny plugged in the drive. Autonomous. An action he had performed too many times to count. Alex watched as windows popped open and screens became populated with a lot of stuff he didn't understand.

'Challenge accepted you little motherfucker!' Manny shouted.

Misha took her seat, trying not to draw attention. Alex didn't react, he heard her unlatching the door. She stepped on a squeaking floorboard. He knew she was heading back not long after she decided to.

Manny spun his chair to face her. 'Last time I had a straight 10 in my house. She wore a balaclava and this nut hit her with a meat hammer!'

She smiled. He had broken the ice.

'I'm gonna need some time to work with this thing, it's as high end as it gets. Your doctor Wally was one smart shitbird.' Manny looked consumed. He often did when he was on the brink of being outsmarted.

'How long?' Alex asked.

'Dude, if I say a week, you'll want it in 5 days.' Manny laughed. 'Gimme 48 hours. I'll have ol Wally's secrets ripe and ready.' Manny turned back to Misha. 'You got any friends? Look as half as good as you? Into guys with their own wheels?' Pointing at the wheels of his chair. The three of them laughed before Alex and Misha said their goodbyes and left.

Chapter 12

'What now?' Misha asked as they drove in his Wrangler. 'I need to take care of something, we need a place to stay also.' He said, focused on the road.

They filled up at a Gas station and grabbed some snacks, toiletries, and some flashlights.

Misha recognised the street as the one she drove Alex to. It looked different in the dark. She knew he was going home and some of the awkwardness she had felt earlier in the evening returned.

Alex came to a stop outside the home he shared with his wife and daughter.

'You can come in if you like.' He said, getting out of the car.

'I don't want to intrude, I'll wait for you, right here.' Misha smiled awkwardly.

He had a quick check of his surroundings. No neighbours curtain twitching. No one walking a dog. He noticed a foreclosure notice stuck the door and ripped it off.

Inside, it lay in the same state, mail scattered behind the door. A layer of dust, undisturbed. There were familiar things all around, but this wasn't his home. He bagged some underwear and other daily items. Stood for a moment, staring at the bed he shared with Sarah. In Emily's room, he took in any lingering scent that was left on her soft toys from her bed. Halfway down the stairs he took a photo off the wall. It was a candid picture, taken of Sarah and Emily on a vacation he couldn't make. It harnessed both the beauty of their relationship but also how happy they were together without him being there. He regretted the time missed out on whilst he fought other men's wars. He removed the photo from the frame as something dropped out from the backing. It caught the air and drifted down to the foot of the steps. He put the picture in his pocket. The piece of paper that fell had something written on it. He used his cell phone to read it in the dark, lifeless house. It read.

Mom. Can daddy come next time.

It was written in Emily's hand. He felt a knot in his stomach and dropped it to the ground. His thoughts came fast, and he felt himself becoming irrational, angry, out of his depth. After a few deep breaths he grounded himself. He walked into the garage and returned to the living room with a jerry can. Doused the sofa and other soft furnishings in fuel before he ignited the note from the photo and tossed it onto the sofa. The flames eating up the fuel as it spread.

Misha noticed the glow from the flames as she watched Alex walk to the car.

'Let's find somewhere to stay.' He said as he drove off from Aspen Gardens for the last time.

He took an evasive route to be sure they weren't followed. 'Any ideas where we should try?' He asked.

'I'd love somewhere with a king size and room service.' She bit her lip, unsure how Alex would respond. 'We could stay in the car if we are keeping a low profile.' She offered.

He passed his cell phone and told her to find a nearby hotel. With a king size.

He passed his key to the valet. His uniform said Greenhills Resort & Spa.

They checked in with a cheery but nightshift weary clerk. 'Room 112 Mr Gray, Mrs Gray. Elevator to the first. Third room on your left. Enjoy your stay.' The man grinned.

He let Misha into the room first and watched her give it the once over. The bed. The bathroom. The massive Tv. He already knew the windows opened out, the exit was a quick 30 feet along the corridor and the door had a double bolt and electronic swipe mechanism.

Misha ordered two Philly Cheesesteak sandwiches and a bottle of red wine on room service. ESPN news played on the Tv. She inspected her face in a mirror. It prompted Alex to check his hand, yellowed fading bruising lingered, and the scabbing was close to falling off. It looked as though it was done a week ago.

He could hear her singing something whilst she showered. A ding of the elevator. Steps getting closer. The rattle of a trolley. Two knocks on the door. He eyed the girl through the peephole before opening. The food and drink had arrived. Another weary night worker. He tipped her twenty and off she went.

Misha returned to the room wearing a hotel robe. Fresh faced. Hair still wet. She fixated her eyes on the food and launched herself on the bed and began to demolish her sandwich. She seemed happy. At Manny's earlier she adjusted well before becoming upset, she fit in. Here, she was undeniably comfortable, enjoying the minor glimpse of normality.

They sat on the bed and drank some wine. Joked about the content playing on ESPN loop. She muted the Tv and performed voice over when the big stars gave an interview. Alex hadn't laughed this much since before the attack.

He had avoided bringing the mood down but felt she should know his plan for the next day. 'Those locations Manny sent. I'm gonna hit one of them tomorrow. The farm and the industrial unit are closest.'

'What do you know about them?' She asked.

'The farm has a lot of traffic. Geo tags from recruitment programmes, meetings, and God knows what else. Worth a look see if I can dig anything up. The unit, not sure, possibly storage or manufacturing purposes.' Alex explained.

'Just tell me what you need me to do.' She smiled, finishing off her glass of wine.

'We can go over it tomorrow.' He poured them each another drink.

A look of mischief in her eye she asked. 'So, you and Manny, did you really get caught sneaking out of base to party?'

He knew what was coming. 'Yeah.' He said smiling and silently cursed Manny.

'How many laps of the base did the C.O make you run?'

'50.' He answered.

'Why did he make you do it naked?' She giggled, taking some pleasure in his discomfort.

'Apparently, two trainee Marines, should not be trying to sleep with the C.O's daughter and her friends.' He conceded, laughing.

'Did you know she set you up?' Misha asked.

'I do now.' Alex emptied his glass in a single gulp.

'I wouldn't have complained.' She said. 'Even in December temperatures.' She winked before giggling.

He now knew Manny had provided full details of their punishment. Manny had a knack for the storytelling. He held embarrassing details like silver bullets.

'Why did you get upset tonight?' He asked her.

'Just overwhelmed, the near-death thing, what has happened to you. John. The things Manny said. Guilt. How I feel about you.' She stopped herself as if she had said too much. 'I'm fine now, sorry.'

'A lot has happened to you, what you had down as normal, as work has been upturned. It's okay to feel overwhelmed.' Alex said. 'You don't need to feel sorry for me.'

Before he could finish Misha spoke again. 'It's not feeling sorry for you. It's having feelings for you. I. I feel so guilty, you have just lost your world and I'm thinking of myself.'

Alex got up and moved their bags and items of clothing to a nearby chair and went for a shower. She noticed something drop to the floor.

When he came back into the room, she was sat looking at the photo of Sarah and Emily.

'She is beautiful. Has your eyes.' She said.

'Yeah, I had to take something to remind me of how they were. After the morgue. The burns. The Arc's insignia carved into them. There was a handwritten note, is Sarah's scrawl, in the backing of the frame. It said The Arc of Evermore.' He dried himself off as he spoke.

'That's weird.' She considered what he had said for a moment. 'Anyone that's made the news related to the Arc are usually tattooed or branded. There's a difference between the two, I think. Those they recruit and those who die in their cause.' She ran a quick search and showed him the official insignia.

It was sort of sickle shaped curve, horizontally, with a Greek style lower case E sitting under it.

They settled in for the night. He offered to sleep on the couch. She reminded him jokingly that it was a king size and lay on the very edge to show how much room there was.

Chapter 13

They left the hotel in the early morning, both armed. The drive to Walker-Mills Farm consisted mostly of winding routes through vast forest, curtained by rolling hills. The time of year offered beautiful contrast of the auburn, yellow and browning leaves, framed by the evergreens. Houses were sparsely dotted between the occasional Ranch. Some looked like working Ranches and some looked like luxury homes.

Walker-Mills looked to be a combination of both. They did a drive by to get a glimpse of the entrance and to scout any nearby service roads. Service roads were usually used by the help for access and egress but also allowed machinery a clear route away from structures and outbuildings.

A gatehouse sat a few hundred metres from the main building. Looked to be staffed by a single guard. A CCTV camera sat on a pole facing the area where vehicles had to stop before the gate. They noticed a service road. Overgrown with vegetation and a few logs sunk into the earth to prevent vehicular access.

Dressed in their tac gear, they parked the car a mile up the road in a layby. It didn't look out of place as it was common for outdoorspeople to park up and go hiking. They used the forest that lined the road and maintained cover until they reached the service road.

'We should head up until we can get a good spot and dig in. Keep eyes on. Look for patterns. Weakness. Points of entry.' Alex kept his voice down.

Several hours had passed. Nobody came or went from the Ranch. Alex was concerned about placing Misha in danger, he planned entrance and exit routes, explained contingency. He sensed her nerves and understood it was normal, but he felt stimulated. Invigorated. Ready for anything.

The sun had dropped behind a neighbouring mountain, and he decided to make his move. Darkness wasn't far away.

'I will go through that door and scout the inside. Intel will do. A computer. Smart device. Anything Manny can hack.' He checked his Glock. 'Anyone comes in behind me, let off a shot, muzzle down. They don't need to know where you are. I'll 180 and head back out. Anyone comes near, they'll need night vision to see you. Stay put and I'll deal with them from my position.' He checked her understanding and headed towards the Ranch.

She watched on, heart pounding in her chest, trying to slow her breathing. She had operated at a high level. Had a reputation as a reputable asset in the private sector. She had never killed a person, no confirmed kills. Many skirmishes and gun battles when looking after the wealthy, the politicians, and Truman's less than transparent assignments. She felt she was capable. Her thoughts drifted to that night at Manny's. Gun pointed at his chest. The truth was that she had no idea what she was going to do when inside that room.

Alex disappeared into a half glass door. He moved like every single step, turn, change in stance was as natural as breathing. He moved as if he had done it a million times over, even when the place was unknown to him. He was special. She knew she would kill for him.

Inside the Ranch, Alex processed the environment like it was a second nature. It was much less extravagant on the inside. The smell of wood, animal hair and open fire smoke dressed the air. Pelts and animal heads dressed furniture and hung-over doorways. Haunting artwork hung on the walls of the hallway. It depicted God like men, lording over naked women and children. It gave him a bad feeling. A baritone voice echoed along the hallway. The words, tailoring off, peaking, some pauses. Some sort of speech he thought.

He headed toward the voice. Using the walls and alcoves to take measure of his surroundings. He stopped intermittently, taking a moment to listen and assess. Whoever it was did not seem to expect an unwanted presence or confrontation. The end of the corridor opened to a large area. It had a small platform, surrounded by small floor mats, a lectern stood upon it. It gave the speaker a strategic vantage point over his audience. Only one man paced the platform. In his 50's. Tall. Excessive curvature of the spine giving him a hunch. He read from a script. The area was too open to get close undetected. He maintained his cover and listened.

'Our chosen. Our subservient. We gather to offer the purest. To select the new chosen. Tonight, we offer blood of the fallen. Tonight, you gather the tears of Jupiter.' The man smiled to himself.

Alex watched as he stepped down and head toward a door at the back of the room. Alex noticed a laptop atop the lectern and made his move.

He had used Manny's device on the laptop and had barely unplugged it when he heard the footsteps. He moved quickly to the doorway and flattened himself against the wall as the door opened.

The man returned with what looked like a medical bag of blood. He mumbled some incomprehensible words as he walked back to the platform. Patchouli oil heavy in the air. A smell Alex held in association with his grandfather, a hippy, wearing it to hide the smell of weed.

Alex, concerned of how exposed he was, standing against the wall, decided the risk was too great to go through the door. If the man turned. He would be seen. Too much ground to cover to silence the man. Shooting him would raise the alarm to anyone lingering and create confusion for Misha. The man's words, although unsure of context, disturbed Alex. He crept closer to the man as he began to speak again.

'Children are our pure. They will serve and nourish us. Allowing path to the Evermore.' He spoke. Holding the blood bag above his head.

That was enough to make Alex decide the next move. Children. Off limits, he thought, this is sick. He got to within a few metres of the man, mounted the platform and in one smooth display of sheer power and momentum, spun the man and released him. He travelled in an almost horizontal fashion through the air. Colliding with a thick supporting pillar headfirst. Alex stood over the man who lay with his head at a 90-degree angle to his neck. A notable indentation to the top of his skull where it made union with the immovable object. Oozing dark red blood. He cloned the man's cell phone and placed it back in the man's pocket.

He listened for any activity and headed back out the way he had come. It was pitch black except semicircles of light cast by sentry lighting around the building.

Misha was relieved to see him emerge from the door. He looked okay, moved faster than earlier, affirmed by a hand gesture in her direction.

'Are you okay?' He asked her.

'Yeah, yeah, what happened?' She said.

'We need to go, same route, I do not know what these freaks are up to, but we need to get clear.' Alex said. He held her hand as they navigated the forest using only the moonlight. Not going too close to the roadside.

In the car, he explained what he heard the man rehearse. She was visibly disgusted.

'Kids are off limits. I need to get this uploaded to Manny.' He spoke as he held the device, he used in one hand. 'I think this is only going to get more messed up.'

As they set off, he noticed Misha was shaking. Sitting in the elements for several hours had caught up with her. He felt bad about going out there under prepared. He turned up the heat and headed back to the hotel.

'Sorry for leaving you out there, I left you unprepared.' Alex said. 'I trust you. I know you have my back.'

'I hope this is true Alex.' She replied.

'It is. I didn't know what was on the other side of that door. I can't lose you too.' Alex checked himself. Felt his face flush. Felt her eyes on him.

'I know the drill, I need to watch your six, cowboy'. She joked. Trying to cull the embarrassment he looked to have felt. A single moment where he didn't measure his words. She wondered if he truly felt at ease around her. 'I don't want to lose you. I want you to know that.' She finished.

Alex's cell phoned buzzed in the centre console. It was Manny.

'You need to come by. I did the thing.' Manny said before ending the call.

Alex and Misha exchanged a nervous glance as he adjusted his route to get to Manny's house.

Chapter 14

They arrived at his house not long after the call. Manny had an expression on his face that deeply unsettled Alex. Knowing something was about to go nuclear, he readied himself and hoped his face could hide any reaction he may be about to have.

'Got the doc's files open.' Manny said as he pointed to one of his screens at what looked like a log or diary entry. 'Seems this guy did whatever Truman told him.'

The earlier entries explained that some sort of testing had been done under lab conditions. A score through each entry represented failure. Waller had detailed some of his inner most thoughts. Mostly regrets pointing toward working for Truman. The last few entries caught Alex's eye:

Another broken soldier arrived today. It's unlike Ed to bring one in personally. This one will never use his arm again or walk without aid. The blood has become poisoned from third party organic tissue becoming embedded. They tell me it was his friends Femur I removed. I give this one three days before incineration.

The latest subject is one A. Brody. More than my predicted time of survival has passed. Ed has asked to initiate another trial. He cares little for my ethics and will surely kill my family should I disobey. I will delay in hope the subject dies.

Not for the first time I am assaulted in my workplace. Ed has truly become unbearable. He has forced the induction of CNS B to the subject. He will surely die like the rest. I sleep very little. I have chosen to become unethical. I have chosen to become yet another plight on humanity.

Alex finished reading from the screen. He remembered the doctor setting up a bag that looked like liquid metal or something. He remembered Truman striking Waller.

'I'm sorry man. I extracted more.' Manny paused. 'CNS B, its Composite Nano Serum B. There were rumours about this stuff. Why Truman was pushed outfield. He was heading up an R&D programme for taking a bit of humanity out of the black ops guys. Eat less. Drink less. Feel less. They say he went too far. His buddy reassigned him.'

'So, he was still doing it? A side hustle?' Alex felt violated. 'Off grid. What the hell did he put into me.'

Manny remained silent and brought up more entries from Dr Waller's pen-drive.

The most positive reaction to the compound we have had to date. The subject has required sedation. The nanomachines have proliferated and are at a doubled count. Pins, plates and screws in the orthopaedic intervention have been disintegrated. Scar tissue heals close to ten times faster than the average male. Reflexes both motor and auditory have shown a ten-fold improvement.

Ed has expressed I communicate with the subject by necessity and to refrain from the news of his wife and daughter. My professional intrigue knows no bounds. It is difficult to keep the subject out of my mind.

I am truly conflicted. In one hand I have played part in the greatest scientific achievement the world will ever see. In the other, I have used my fellow man as a lab rat, I have acted against the core design of being a doctor. I have allowed a terrorist to dictate over me. Money. A free reign. No restrictions. Was it worth it?

The subject has spent three months in bed. Induced sedation multiple times. CNS B proliferation decreased. Maintains muscle mass. Organ tissue regenerated from any trauma. Scan shows some calcification in the temporal region. Same as 99% of the others. So why, how has he survived his peers?

A cold bead of sweat ran from his neck and down his back. He understood why Manny had worn that expression on his face.

Staring at the floor Alex finally spoke. 'I'm Truman's pet, his success story.'

Misha, concern on her face, stood and tentatively walked to Alex. 'What is it?'

'Did you know?' He said.

'About what?' She asked.

Alex nodded to the screen and walked into the kitchen.

She took a few minutes to read the entries Manny had brought up.

'How much more is there?' She asked Manny.

'Plenty, these ones relate to Alex, the others. Are the disappeared.' Manny said as he scrolled the files.

'This is why he had us hitting his own site.' Misha continued. 'Cleaning house, fucking snake!'

'I'll deal with him later. Let him think he holds all the cards.' Alex returned, composed, beer in hand for the three of them.

Misha did her best to hide any pity that could be wrongly interpreted by Alex. Her dark eyes, strangely emotive given their tone could betray her.

'What do you have on the Arc?' Alex asked Manny and pointed to the cloning device he left on the desk.

'Nothingman.' Manny said.

'What? You are joking, right? I cloned the computer and cell phone.' Alex said. He felt his anger building inside.

'No, no. You, it's what they are calling you.' Manny said as he pulled up correspondence from the cloned devices. 'You are the Nothingman. A man with nothing. No limits. A kite without a string.'

'They know about me, how?' He asked.

'They were sent an encrypted message, here.' Manny pointed.

On the screen it read:

The Nothingman is coming.

'This got pinged to at least a dozen different cells, IP addresses, you name it.' Manny said. 'A warning.'

'Truman.' Both Alex and Misha said in tandem.

'Find anything you can on Clark. He worked with Waller at the site. I need some answers.' Alex said.

'There's something else man.' Manny said. 'Dude whose laptop you did. A deacon for the Arc. Jacket as long as my dreads. Cruelty. Paedophilia. Abduction. You name it. He dead?'

Alex looked at him. 'He's dead.'

Alex knew why Manny was invested in the details and wished his friend had an easier childhood.

'They are preying on women and children, man.' Manny continued. 'Several sources, the internet and some police reports they claim they harvest the blood of children in their pursuit of evermore. One woman claimed she was held and forced to birth three children. They took them for the elders.'

'Fuck, what did the police do?' Alex asked.

'She was strung out on H by the time she got to em. She's in a psychiatric unit upstate.' Manny said as he shook his head.

'Can you collate as much of this stuff as possible?' Alex asked, but before Manny could answer. 'Not the Truman stuff.'

Manny nodded.

'Got a media contact?' He asked.

Again, Manny nodded and worked his cell phone. Alex felt his own cell buzz in his pocket. They left Manny working his magic and started back to the Greenhills Hotel and Spa.

He felt Misha's eyes bore into him as he drove. 'How can you hold it together? This is beyond rational comprehension. I knew the government did things but this. I don't even know what to say.' She said.

'He is working outside the government. Using people to prove a point. Getting upset now will only hinder my progression.' Alex said, assured, confidently.

'Do you think it's dangerous, what they put in you?' She asked.

'The part about the calcification in my head.' He paused thinking he would cause her to worry. 'That headache the other night at Manny's. Same spot. Second time.'

'We should take you to a doctor, what if it gets worse?' Her breathing becoming faster.

'I will. I promise. I need to deal with the Arc of Evermore first.' Alex winked at her, concealing his angst.

He stood in the bathroom of their room staring at the wounds he had brought back from the middle east. The scars. More subtle than any other man would wear after that night. Healed by nanotechnology. He thought about his way of assessing threat. Planning for a fast exit. His hearing. The small things he noticed. A tiny inflection in someone's voice signalling a red flag. All down to the tiny things coursing through his body, making faster connections, helping the cells do their work. He remembered reading about the use of Amphetamines, LSD and other substances used in trying to get more out of your frontline operatives.

'Alex.' Misha called out from the room.

He snapped out of it and took a seat on the bed. She stood with the room service menu. He chose a club sandwich and asked for a beer.

As they ate, the news reporter announced a death in the hierarchy of the Arc of Evermore. A request to parade the late Deacon Vernon Klinger was refused by city officials citing a conflict in public interest. The reporter signed off by stating the Arc of Evermore refused to comment on the speculation surrounding their practices of child exploitation and abuse.

'That him?' Misha asked.

'Yeah.' Alex took a pull on his beer. 'Kids are off limits.'

Alex startled Misha by reaching for his gun. Holding his finger to his lips he ushered her to get down.

His ears picked up slow, measured footsteps, they were coming along the corridor. Boots. Not service staff. He looked at the clock. 01:09am. It was too late to shut off the lights. They were outside.

Misha flattened herself to the floor as Alex grabbed a bathrobe. He used the separating wall of the bathroom as cover as he peered around to the door. He could see the shadow cast by the person's legs under the door. Two quiet knocks. A pause. A folded piece of paper slipped under the door. The legs didn't move. They still stood in situe.

Alex held out the bathrobe at arm's length from his cover. A loud pop erupted in the room. Splinters of wood from the door flying through the air. The robe swept out of his grasp.

The unmistakable click-clack of a shotgun being breeched.

Again. Another blast ripping through the air, and another. Glass breaking from the spread of the pellets. Feathers from the bedding floating in the air.

He thought about blind firing around the corner and decided against it. There could be anyone in the room behind the shooter. He heard footsteps again. Faster. This time getting father away. He vaulted the bed to where Misha lay.

'I'm okay, I'm okay!' She said. He quickly ran his hands over her. A sweep to identify active bleeding. To make sure she was okay. 'Get everything you can. We need to move.' Screeching tyres filled the air outside the broken window as he spoke to her.

She was shaking as she tossed anything that wasn't already in the bag into it.

Alex scooped up the piece of paper as he passed the door. It hung open with three dinner plate sized holes in it. Glock at chest height. He cleared the corridor. Misha at his back with her weapon drawn.

They took the stairs to avoid being caught in the elevator. A bottleneck was easy for anyone trying to take out a mark. Just point and shoot. Keep shooting. Nowhere to go.

As they passed the reception desk the night manager stood smiling at them. The screen next to him was blank. The cctv system was off. A rage simmered inside Alex.

'Did you tell them what room I was in?' Alex shouted as Misha tugged his wrist to go.

'The Arc of Evermore thanks you for your custom.' The man said Holding up his wrist to show the crescent and E symbol.

'Ah fuck you.' Alex shouted as they left. He knew they were vulnerable. Misha was right to try get him moving.

They got to his car. He started the engine. Misha expected him to drive but he reached into the glove box and removed the carpenter's hammer.

Shirtless. Dressed only in a pair of shorts he got out the car. A look in his eye that could not be bargained with.

'Please wait here.' He said to Misha.

The man stood smiling at the desk until he saw the hammer in Alex's hand. The smile washed off as Alex stepped closer.

Alex returned to his car empty handed. He drove quickly, making sure they didn't have a tail.

'Did he say anything?' Misha asked.

'No, he recited something similar to the Deacon.' Alex said. 'Suppose they can share stories together in hell now.'

'The cell.' Misha said. 'The one Truman gave you; you think he's tracking us?'

'Testing out his new product. Maybe.' Alex said.

As he drove, he considered the possibility that Truman was behind it.

He found a track off the main road that split the forest the Greenhills resort was part of.

'Might need to get some sleep here. Until its light at least.' Alex said as he assessed the surroundings and killed the engine. 'Wrap up, it's gonna be cold.'

He unfolded the piece of paper from the room. It read.

I See You.

Handwritten. Watermarked. A napkin from Duke's bar.

They slept in the car. Dawn approached quicker than they expected. A cold, uncomfortable night ended by birds chirping and a low sun beaming through the windows.

'What do we do now?' Misha asked.

'The industrial unit. Need to go see what is going on.' Alex continued. 'Somebody has warned them. Soon as they know the Hotel hit went wrong, they could start to shut up or move.'

They grabbed coffee and a breakfast on the road.

'Cuba.' He said.

'What?' Misha said.

'When this is over.' Alex reached over and held her hand as he drove. 'We should go to Cuba. When this is over.'

'Where you go. I'll go.' She replied. 'If you'll have me.'

A comfortable silence consumed the rest of the drive. Misha checked her weapon several times. A sign of how nervous she was. Alex had learned this over the last few days.

A medium sized industrial unit. Could have been a production factory or storage site. It was impossible to tell from the outside. They watched from a distance as trucks entered and exited the site. Unmarked. Controlled entry. An armed guard in a legitimate looking uniform. Alex could not assume there wouldn't be more inside. It was late morning. Going in quiet was the only option.

After another drive by. He knew the south of the site was the best option. He found it strange there was an armed guard and no cctv. The Arc weren't ordinary people though, he thought.

'If he leaves the gate, I need you at his back. He will shoot either of us on sight.' Alex briefed Misha. 'We need each other as contingency. There is no time to prep or recon.'

'Got it.' Misha said.

Alex left her at their vantage point across from the gate and made his way around the chain link fence to the south.

He scaled the fence and used shipping containers as cover to get closer to the building. The hum of a diesel engine passed close to where he crouched. The rattle of a chain as a roller door dropped back to the ground. He moved towards a rusted metal fire escape stairwell. The bolts into the brick surrounded by cracks and rust stains. He made his way up to the first floor. He felt like he was being watched as he used his knife to break the escape door mechanism.

Misha sat in the car and noticed a dark figure heading along the same route Alex did. The area was a reasonably accessible site and was home to several businesses. It wouldn't be uncommon to see someone trying a shortcut. When the man turned and raised his hand to his mouth, speaking, she knew something was off. Her suspicion confirmed when he swung out a shotgun from his coat and dropped into a tactical stance, heading after Alex.

Alex found himself on a steel catwalk when he entered. Rows of rooms without ceilings rand the length of the building below him. He felt sick at what he saw. Most of the rooms were filled with women. They were all bound to beds or chained to metal rings bolted to the floor. Some of the women were pregnant. Some nursed babies. Some looked dead. The metallic smell of blood filled the air. What looked like a nurse wheeled a trolley along the corridor with medical style bags of what he assumed to be blood. He slowly moved along the catwalk to the opposite end taking in the horrors that were below. What he seen did not get any less disturbing. The final room had an elderly man sitting in a chair hooked up to an IV line. A bag of blood flowing into his veins. He immediately thought about the words the Deacon had said. The blood of the children. He took some photos on his cell phone from his vantage point as he moved.

He unholstered his gun and crept down the internal stairwell. He knew the door would lead to the corridor and the first room had the old guy in it. He quietly entered the room where the man slept in a reclining chair. He saw the insignia on the right wrist of the man. Anytime he saw it, he remembered Emily laying on the slab. The old man would have never known how he met his end. Alex quickly wrapped his arms around his neck and snapped it with a violent twist. The man exhaled as he left the waking world.

In the next room lay a woman. In her twenties he guessed. He held his finger to his mouth to keep her quiet when she saw him. She wore a tattered nightdress. She was pale, tired looking, a recent black eye shadowed her left eye. He felt a tightness in his throat when he noticed the branding in the centre of her chest. Scabbed. Dry. A reminder of a horror this human being had endured.

'Hey, I'm not one of them. I'm going to try get you some help.' He whispered, untying the leather strap from her neck.

'Where's my baby? They took him.' She said, through cracked lips. Her eyes told him she knew but didn't want to believe it. He looked into her eyes and wondered if he looked the same to her, a void, something missing, never to return.

The squeaking of the trolley alerted him. The nurse. He thought.

He took cover inside the doorway as it got closer. He sprung from his cover when it passed the door. No one was there. He quickly spun around expecting to see the nurse. Instead, it was a tall man. Dressed in black. Shotgun pointed at his chest. The shooter from the Hotel, he thought.

'The Nothingman.' The man smiled, gesturing for Alex to look behind him.

He already heard them approaching and turned to confirm. The nurse stood, chains and restraints in hand. The guard from the gate, gun holstered, baseball bat in hand.

As he turned to face the man holding the shotgun. He heard the noise before he felt any pain. Across his shoulder blades. It knocked him to his knees.

'And again Lucius.' The shotgun wielding man ordered.

Alex braced himself for another hit but instead he saw the muzzle flash from above. Crack. Crack. The sound of footsteps along the catwalk. Getting closer.

The shotgun hit the floor before the man did. He twitched a little and Alex could see two holes in the top of his head.

He turned as the guard fumbled his gun. The nurse swung the chains at Alex and turned on her heels towards the staircase. Alex raised his gun and fired twice. He made sure to hit him around the mouth. If he wore a vest he might still hit Alex, this way he was dead before his brain could sent the signal to shoot.

The nurse let out a shriek from inside the stairwell. Two more cracks. She rolled backwards down the stairs. Coming to a stop at the bottom. Blood spreading across her tunic. The look of fright slowly fading from her face as her muscle tone loosened and death became her.

Alex was still on his knees as Misha exploded from the stairwell. She rushed to him.

'Hey, hey, you alright? Are you hurt?' She gave him a once over. 'I'm sorry, I should have been faster. I ....' She stopped as she took in the horrors around her.

He pulled her in close. 'We need to get these people some help.' He said.

After he cloned the cell phones of the dead, He dialled 911 from one of them and muted the mic.

'We need to go.' Urgency in his voice.

'Wait, we can untie these girls.' Misha said. Tears in her eyes as she absorbed her surroundings.

'No, we need to go, now, they'll send Paramedics with the Police.' He held her face and looked into her eyes. 'We have done enough here.'

He wished the shotgun wielding man was alive enough to have gotten some information from him. He held nothing against Misha. She saved his life. It had to happen this way.

They walked briskly, to the car to avoid drawing any attention from passing motorists.

'That woman. I saw the whites of her eyes. That scream.' Misha's voice trembled.

Alex pulled her head in close. 'She would have killed either of us. You did what was necessary. I'd be dead right now if it wasn't for you.'

'It's different than being in a firefight. You rarely know when you have gotten a kill. It's about getting your VIP out. Safe. Quickly.' Misha added.

'The guy with the shotgun. That's twice he has found us. Somebody is feeding them information.' Alex angrily said.

Misha got him to lean forward as he drove. She pulled up his top, revealing a reddened lesion the width of his back. He heard her try and stifle a gasp.

'It's fine. It'll be gone soon if what Waller reported is true.' He said.

'Does it hurt though?' She asked.

'Oh yeah it does, the healing was the standard package. Feeling no pain was the upgrade.' He laughed.

Alex pulled out the cell phone Truman had given him and dialled the number. There was no answer. No option to leave a message. Alex annoyed with the idea that only two people knew where they were, or at least possessed means of finding out. The cell phones, he thought. He put it to the back of his mind. For now.

He pulled in at a gas station. Fuelled up and bought two burner phones, and some snacks and water. They sat in the car by the roadside. Misha set up her new burner whilst Alex scanned the classifieds for somewhere to rent.

Misha jumped as he spoke. 'Hi, my name is Joel and I am interested in renting your property on Maple park.' A pause. 'Yeah, yeah, no, that's fine. Okay two months up front is not a problem.' Another pause. 'Cash. Non-smoker. No pets.' Alex looked at his GPS. 'One hour'. He ended the call.

'So, we don't talk about these things anymore? You just go ahead and rent a house, without talking to me!' She gave her act away easily. Laughing.

'Pass me that Ziplock bag. No one can know where we are going.' He said.

Misha perused the classified listing as Alex drove. It was a semi-remote location. A cabin on the edge of a state forest. A single road in. A lounge, kitchen, one bedroom and a bathroom.

'Cosy.' She offered.

He pulled up by a road marker. Around 2 miles from the concealed road that would take them to the property. Misha got out to stretch her legs. Alex pulled a foldaway shovel from the trunk and dug a hole in the earth. He tossed the Ziplock bag, the cell phones sealed inside, into the hole and filled it in. He took a couple of the rolled-up bundles of cash and counted out a few thousand dollars, made a single fold and stuffed them into his pocket.

They both carefully surveyed the single-track road that led to the cabin. Nothing unusual. Few signs of regular foot or vehicular traffic.

As they pulled up outside. A minivan was parked outside. Alex spotted the man sitting on a bench in the porch. Thin. Wiry. Outdoorsman aura about him. Had to be at least sixty. The man spoke as soon as Alex stepped out the Jeep.

'Joel. I assume.' He shouted.

'Yes, sir, Joel Gray. Thank you for allowing us to come up and view your property.' He replied.

'You, military, son?' The man asked.

'Once upon a time, sir.'

'Army Rangers, myself.' The man continued. 'Earl Nash, how do you do?' He reached out and shook Alex's hand. 'That your little lady in the vehicle?'

Alex beckoned Misha out the car, and she joined them. Earl introduced himself. Apologised several times for profanity when explaining how his knees had betrayed him. He gave them a tour.

'I can't get up here much these days. If my damn knees belonged to a horse, they'd shoot me. There's a leak in the roof, around where the bathroom is. You fix it up and I'll give you it half price.' He pointed at a large cabinet in the lounge. 'There's a 12 gauge and a Winchester lever action in there. Keys atop. It'll stop a normal bear and scare off one of them big asshole ones.'

'Earl, I'll tell you what.' Alex spoke. 'No discount, I'll fix the roof. Keep it off the books and I'll pay you six months' rent. Upfront.'

The old man studied Alex for a second. 'Okay.' He walked to the kitchen and pulled out a dusty bottle of Pappy Van Winkle bourbon. 'I never make a deal without a drink, son.' He poured three drinks and knocked his own back in a single gulp. 'You use em guns on anything but a bear. They can't be traced. You know what I'm saying.'

Alex handed him the money and Earl handed him the key.

'Call me if you wanna extend your rental.' Earl said as he walked out the door. He got into his minivan and left.

Both Alex and Misha smiled at the unique charm Earl Nash had about him.

Chapter 15

Alex was up on the roof replacing a couple of boards and resetting the shingle within the hour. Misha changed out the bedding and made coffee.

'If you told me this, was it. We could just stay here. Not be bothered by anyone, I'd have bitten your hand off.' Misha said as she watched Alex climb back down off the roof.

'Yeah. A cabin in the woods. It does something to a person.' Alex continued. 'It grounds you. Surrounded by the trees. The smells. The birds. If there was a lake view, I'd have bought it from Earl.'

They sat in silence for the next half hour. On the porch, drinking their second coffee. A squirrel ambled close enough before being spooked by the call of a bird nearby.

'Truman hands me a cell phone. The shooter finds us twice.' Alex said out loud, subconsciously stroking his beard. 'Why warn the Arc that I'm coming if I am the monster he created?'

'Alex, monster. Seriously?' Misha said resentful of that term.

'We are off grid, for the time being. I'd say we stay out of the limelight for a day. See what gets reported from today.' Alex said.

'Here, have a look.' Misha passed her phone. It was an article from the same journalist they saw on the news the other night.

Over a dozen women and children saved in morning raid during a Police operation in the manufacturing district. A source has reported that the Arc of Evermore have been linked to the site where several people were found shot to death. Police have refused to comment on an ongoing investigation at this time.

'Why aren't they telling the world what happened to those women? Those babies?' Misha was disgusted.

'I hope it's a process thing. Evidence gathering.' Alex said. 'Could be that they are protecting them.'

He got up and moved his car to where Earl's vehicle sat. So that it wouldn't be seen if anyone approached. At least until they were in front of the cabin. A clear line of sight.

Exactly as Earl had said. The shotgun and rifle sat, fully loaded in the cabinet. No serial numbers. Alex laughed to himself. He lit the fire using the kindling that sat in a nearby basket. He thought about how far the woodshed was from the rear door of the cabin. A shotgun spraying its projectiles would hit anyone coming from the cabin. He told Misha that where she should go if they have uninvited guests. He would double back and neutralise any threat from the forest.

He sat in front of the fire. The occasional crackle sending out a red-hot ember to the stone that separated the fire from the timber boards. The red fading away when there was no fuel left to keep it alive. This is what he would do the Arc of Evermore, put out their light, so they can't hurt another soul. The thought of who had given the gunman their locations still ate away at him.

'The noise of the fire always reminds me of my better spent youth. Beach in sunny California. Feet in the sand. Bottle of beer.' Misha's voice, interrupting his thoughts, he was grateful. 'Right before I decided I needed to move to the other side of the country. Find a bad ass man and take down a cult.'

They both laughed. She nudged his arm, holding a glass of Earl's bourbon out to him.

He thought about the circumstances in which they met.

'How's the arm?' He asked.

'Feels better, well, less painful, might try without the splint tomorrow.' She replied. 'Holding my weapon isn't easy, control of recoil before the second shot hurts like hell.'

'There's a reason I left my hammer back at the Greenhills.' Alex said through a burst of laughter.

She side-eyed him for a second before rolling herself over him, pinning him on his back.

'I don't need a hammer.' She looked down on him. Biting her lip as she moved her head closer.

She kissed him. This time he didn't try to break away.

She straddled him and pulled her top off over her head. He remembered how he felt seeing her body back the Motel. Before he could, Misha removed his shirt. He pulled her close. Kissing her. His heart beating hard, against his chest. He rolled her until he was on top of her. She bit his lip and began to remove her jeans. He took her right there on the floor. The crackling fire drowned out by their moans.

They lay under a blanket for a while. Misha felt apprehensive to move away or look up from where she rested her head on his chest, it was in case, she saw regret on his face.

Alex, lay there, he thought about the future, if there was a future for him and Misha. He held her a little longer before kissing the top of her head.

'Fancy some food?' He asked.

'Thought you'd never ask.' She replied.

They shared a shower whilst some pasta sat simmering in a pan.

Earl's bottle of Van Winkle bourbon didn't stand a chance. They emptied it over dinner. He studied her face. Her manner. Her casual use of sarcasm that made light of an outlandish scenario they both were living. She had stopped people from killing him, and in the process had to kill them herself. He had nothing, but owed her everything. He told himself that he would do anything to protect her, that if one of them was to come out of this, alive and well, it would be her.

He was mid conversation, topping up the wood on the fire when he felt it. The ringing in the ears. The stabbing in the temporal region of his head.

'C'mon Alex.' He heard her voice before he opened his eyes.

She was crouched over him, holding a wet towel over his head. The fire still burning behind her.

'I'm sorry.' He said as he sat up.

'That was longer than last time.' Misha said, holding him. Her face wore the stress of what she had just witnessed.

'I'll see if Manny has found anything of the other doctor, he might know if this can be stopped.' He said.

'Yeah, tomorrow, lets get you to bed.' Misha told him.

He noticed that his gun was already by the bed. Misha's too. He could hear her locking up the external doors. Checking windows and drawing any blinds.

He slept better that night than the many nights before. He woke once, around 03:00am and checked the surroundings outside the cabin. Deathly quiet. The occasional creaking tree breaking the silence. The darkness of the forest reminded him of the desert. Without artificial light you couldn't see your hand in front of you at arm's length. He returned to bed. Misha stirred and he kissed her forehead.

He was up first. He had just about plated up some scrambled eggs and salsa as she walked in from the bedroom.

'Oww, could get used to this.' She smiled and eyed her steaming cup of coffee like a vulture eyeing its prey.

'You like this? Just wait till dinner, I found more bourbon.' He joked as he ate his breakfast.

'I'm gonna take a walk down to the marker. See if anyone has been looking for us. I can check the cells for anything from Manny or Truman.' Alex said as he got up.

'Okay, call if you need me to come down.' Misha said, clearing the table.

Alex walked down the single-track road. Scanning for any signs that anyone had been snooping around. He decided to stay within the tree line that ran alongside the road towards the marker. He didn't want to be seen or bothered by anyone. He carried only a rucksack with his folding shovel and his knife. If he was seen or stopped by any law enforcement, it was easier to explain these items. An un-registered firearm with no serial number could get him arrested or shot.

As he walked, he could smell the musky odour of something, maybe an elk or other similar animal. It would have smelled him well before he could even comprehend it being nearby. He spotted tracks in the brush and some droppings. Without a gun, he was relieved it was a hoofprint and not a bear track.

He thought about the times his old man would bring him to the forest. They'd fish and hunt. His father would press him to remember his own ethos, only take what you can eat. He knew he hadn't taken Emily out enough. He could count on one hand how many times they went out in the wild. It wasn't that she didn't like it, she did. The treks, taking out a canoe on a lake and toasting marshmallows over a fire were her most favourite things to do. The hunting, the fish, not so much. His mind drifted to Sarah. How she just got on with doing the job of two parents whilst he was away. He knew he was failing them both, could see it happening, he should have gotten out when she had asked him to. One more deployment, his answer.

He should have seen it sooner, amongst his regrets was that he became a part time dad, a part time husband. He understood the type of work he done wasn't normal, that the ripple effect would continue until the day he died. Possibly after. He lost a little part of himself every single day he put on that uniform; he knew it deep down. Every time he got home, he spent the first few days angry, unable to sleep, visiting the drinks cabinet too often. By the time he had grounded himself, decompressed, it was always too late. Time to go back.

A gentle rain had begun as he walked. He stopped, to listen. The sloshing sound made by the tyres of passing drivers, the rhythmical beats each droplet made when caught by the leaves of the trees. He didn't mind the rain. He found it relaxing, the regular tapping on the roof tiles of home or the tent he was using when working, it didn't matter. It made sense to him, that everything around him needed it, it topped up the streams that ran underfoot, washed away the red and orange and brown leaves cast off by the branches above. It renewed, provided nourishment, and changed how things were seen.

The screech of tyres then a dull thud stopped him moving.

Alex crouched and listened. He knew he could not be seen from where he had heard the noises. Two gunshots and some shouting filled the air. Again, the screeching of tyres as a vehicle sped past where he took cover.

He made sure it was clear and stepped out on the road. As he looked toward where the vehicle had come from, he saw the form of a deer. It was dragging itself toward the treeline. As he got closer, he noticed the little rivulet by the roadside, caused by the rain running red. The deer paid no attention to him as he approached. Its hind legs splayed in the most unnatural manner. He could tell by its size, it was young, emaciated and even before today, would not survive the winter.

Alex scooped the dying animal up from the road and walked into the forest. When he placed it down on the soft earth, padded with pine needles and leaves, it didn't move or try to get away. He looked into its large black eye, blinking as its heavy laboured breath pushed out some frothy pink bubbles from its nose. He stroked the animal's neck gently. He saw two bullet holes, one in the gut and another on its rump.

He thought about his father as he lay dying, lungs no longer able to absorb the oxygen he craved. Complications from Vietnam they said, he blamed the agent orange and the phosphorous. His father had told him, if he was ever going to kill, it should be in mercy, or in a fight for your life itself. He pushed the blade of his knife into the base of the animal's skull. It made no noise, no movement, and only closed its large eyes as if it had simply drifted to sleep.

The next twenty minutes was spent shovelling dirt as he dug a grave for the animal. He felt it was the right thing to do and cursed the driver for prolonging the suffering the animal had to endure.

Drops of rain ran down his face, into his beard as he reached the roadside marker. No disturbance underfoot. No vehicle tracks could be the rain washed them away or that no one had stopped by. He quickly retrieved the cell phones and disappeared back into the cover of the forest.

The cell that Truman had given him had no calls or messages. The other, that Manny had provided had a missed call and text message. It was from Manny:

AB. Found your man. Call me.

It rang twice after he dialled Manny's number.

'Hey, what's the matter? You screen my calls?' Manny asked.

'No. Went off grid for a day. What do you have?' Alex said.

'I seen the thing on the news. Ain't much been said bout the Arc man. This why you want a reporter involved?'

'Manny, we can talk when I see you, I have more data on your gadget thing. What have you got on Clark?'

'He's alive and well. Doing a guest spot at Belle Isle University tomorrow. Could go grab him.' Manny finished.

'I'll drop by today.' Alex said ending the call.

Misha was sat in front of the fire as he returned. Soaked by the rain, he stood just inside the door as he removed his boots and outer layers.

'Hey.' Some concern in her eyes. 'Didn't expect you to be gone that long. Are you good?'

'Of course, I'm fine, Manny has something for us on Clark.' He flicked on the coffee machine. 'Could you run a quick search on Belle Isle university, maybe include the name Dr Clark.'

He noticed the exact moment she saw the blood on his hand.

'It's not mine, or anyone else's for that matter. Some jackass hit a deer with their car, shot it, and I ended its suffering, buried it.' Alex explained. 'I'm gonna clean myself up and get something a little less wet on. Will you be good to go soon?'

'Sure.' She typed into her cell phone.

When he returned, she tossed her phone for him to read what she had found. It was an advertisement for the University.

Award winning Dr Winston Clark will be at Belle Isle University to deliver a guest seminar this week! He is a leading expert in experimental genetic engineering and has a resume that includes some of the biggest achievements in the field. His recent work with the U.S government .....

It tailed off discussing what the public were permitted to know about some project he had been part of for Uncle Sam.

'He got a family?' Alex asked.

'Yeah, wife, three kids.' She replied.

'That's how we get close to him.' Alex said.

Misha's face did not betray what she thought Alex had meant.

'No, no, he only needs to think we have them.' He said, palms up, disarming her.

Chapter 16

It took an hour to reach Manny's place. He retrieved the cell phones from the roadside marker on the way. The rain had continued most of the drive.

Manny sat in his usual spot, in front of his workstation, making things appear, vanish and switch from one screen to another of the six.

'Where'd you go? Yesterday?' Manny asked. 'Thought you'd gotten got! Or arrested.'

'Just needed a moment away from it all, that's all.' Alex handed him the cloning device.

Manny plugged it in and typed in some commands before wheeling himself into the kitchen.

'He treating you alright, girl?' Manny addressed Misha. 'I might be in a chair, but I'll beat his ass if he ain't. Told your friends about me yet?' He returned, eating some jerky.

'Manny, you know I only have eyes for you.' Misha joked, 'Besides, my friends are all in LA, I'll take you across to meet them one day, maybe after all this craziness is over.'

A tone signalled the upload of the device, Manny worked his way back to his machines.

'Something you need to know Mr Nothingman.' Manny was getting his kicks with the name Alex had attracted by his recent exploits. 'You are hitting the right places, The Arc have put a million dollars on your head..'

'How do you know this?' Alex asked.

'Dark web chatter. It's how they organise their recruitment, events blah blah. Y'know.' Manny said. 'They have no idea who you are anyway. You don't exist, remember.'

'Getting anything from the people I ran into at the industrial unit?' Alex asked.

'Nah, drained their accounts though, one was an elder, addressed as if he were royal or some shit in any messages he received.' Manny laughed. 'What's next man? You hitting up the last location I got you?'

'Not yet. I need to speak to Clark. Then Truman.' Alex said. 'Has Harvey Jupiter popped his head out yet?'

'No, man, keep hitting his places, he will show up soon, if he's putting down a mill already, it's working.' Manny said.

An unfamiliar tone chirped in the room. Alex grabbed his jacket and pulled out the cell phone Truman had given him. It was ringing.

He pressed the green accept call button.

'Brody. What part of I call you, don't you quite get? You are lucky I like you.' Truman could be heard taking a pull on a cigar, a slight cough. 'Marty and Moe's diner. Thirty minutes.' The phone went dead.

He looked at Misha. They spoke with their eyes. She knew it was Truman. The look on her face confirmed this much.

'Truman wants to meet. Thanks brother, keep doing what you are doing.' He said to Manny, putting on his jacket.

Walking to the car, he asked Misha. 'You wanna stay away from him, I get it, no need to put you in front of him again.'

'I'm part of this, I'll be fine.' She replied, irked by his suggestion.

They drove to the diner in less than Truman's time scale. He was already there. Alex could see him sat at a booth from the parking lot. A blacked-out SUV sat idling outside. He couldn't tell who, or how many people were inside. Truman looked relaxed as they walked across the lot towards the entrance. Alex knew an operator like Truman would have known they were approaching before they had even entered the lot. He hadn't gotten to where he was without due diligence.

They entered the diner; a waitress greeted them. She made way for them to pass as they told her they were meeting the gentleman at the back.

'Brody.' Truman greeted him. He didn't acknowledge Misha. 'Seen you've been busy. Has my info been of any help?'

'Yeah, feels a little bit like you wind me up, and let me go.' Alex answered.

'There's an envelope in that menu.' He gestured with his chin, as he cleaned his glasses with a napkin. 'You will find what is inside, interesting.'

Alex pulled out the envelope and opened it.

Truman turned to Misha. 'Look, it seems you aren't going away. If we are going to have to work together.' He placed his glasses back on, prolonging the pause. 'I'm sorry I struck you. I stand corrected in my thinking that John was the better asset.' He sipped a black coffee. 'He needs you. I need him. You are off limits.'

Misha just nodded when he had finished. She held a hatred for Truman that wasn't about to just go away.

Alex looked through the papers that were inside the envelope. He knew Truman was staring a hole through him, trying to read him.

'You know they have a price on you?' Truman said.

'Yep, a waste of a million dollars don't you think?' Alex said, looking up at Truman. Looking for a hint that he was playing games.

Truman laughed. His cigar and coffee breath wafted towards Alex and Misha. 'Fucking fuck the man who comes up against you kid.'

'They can come for me if they want. One thing is guaranteed though.' Alex stuffed the papers back inside the envelope.

'What's that?' Truman scoffed.

'They'll stop when I cut the head off the snake.' Alex smiled at Truman. Wondering what game, he was playing. Who's side he was on. He thought about the potential for Truman to be enjoying this.

'Kid, Misha. Do what is necessary.' Truman brushed his shirt with his hands as he stood. He slapped a fifty-dollar bill down on the table and left.

They ordered a couple of waffles with bacon and coffee.

'What did he give you?' Misha asked.

'I need to find out more before I can explain any of it.' Alex held her hand. 'It looks like they have cops on the payroll or in the ranks of The Arc.'

After lunch, Misha drove them to Belle Isle University campus. They held hands as they walked through the grounds. They looked as though they'd done it a hundred times, no attention paid to them by anyone. Sat on a bench at a water fountain, they assessed their surroundings. The signs advertising Clark's seminar were spread throughout the area.

The building that was to be used had good access and egress from the neighbouring parking lot.

'Any idea how we get him?' Alex asked. 'He will surely recognise me. It would be difficult for me to get close in the public view.'

'I'll get close to him.' Misha smiled. 'Besides, I look younger than you, I'll blend right in.' She laughed.

Alex drove them to a nearby Motel. They paid for a night.

Chapter 17

The Belle Isle campus was as busy as you would expect. Students shuttling between buildings. The parking lot filled and emptied like a sped-up time lapse of the tide. They spent the latter part of the morning and early afternoon watching the goings on. Campus cops covered their patrol routes in a golf cart. Too consumed in their own little bubble to notice Alex and Misha.

Alex spotted the weasel like Clark as soon as he arrived. He was quick in getting out the car and into the building. Dressed in a three-piece suit, brogue shoes and carrying a laptop bag he looked every part the legitimate leading edge of science. Misha kissed Alex and got out of the car.

'Wish me luck.' She winked and headed towards the building.

Inside the large lecture hall, Clark was introduced by the Dean. He spoke as he clicked through a presentation for the best part of thirty minutes. Misha conceded that she knew very little of what he had spoken about.

Another fifteen minutes of questions concluded the seminar. She thought he spoke well, very passionate about his work but she was bored. She sat in silence hoping the students would stop asking questions.

Finally, he was applauded off the stage and made his way up the centre aisle. She excused herself from the person sitting between her and the aisle. She managed to get out as he passed and headed out to the lobby.

'Dr Clark.' She called after him.

'Yes.' He turned to see who had said his name.

'What an honour it is to have been able to listen to your seminar.' She smiled.

'Oh you are too kind Miss.' He was about to speak again until she continued.

'Please could sign my ticket, I have it right here.' Misha held it out.

'Of course.' He smiled taking the ticket from her.

'Who do I make it out to?' He asked, pen poised, looking down at the ticket.

'Well, it should say, we have your wife and three kids, and it would be best for them if you come with me.' She stood smiling as if it were a completely normal thing to say. Any bystander would have assumed she complimented him as she smiled and spoke.

He slowly looked up from the ticket. His eyes met Misha's as she read the terror inside of him.

'There's a black Jeep Wrangler in the lot. You take your little self on out there. There is someone waiting to speak to you.' She said, as he opened his mouth to speak. She held a finger up causing him to stand there, mouth open, silent. 'Shout, try to make a call, do anything other than what I have asked. I'll send a text and it's all over.'

Alex was rolling his neck and stretching out as he saw Clark walking out the building. Followed by Misha. He could see the weasel looking man scan the lot until he spotted the Jeep.

Clark sat in the passenger seat on direction and Misha jumped in the back seat. The look on his face when he saw Alex was one of sheer confusion, shock, then fear.

'Expecting someone else Clark?' Alex asked, smiling at the little man.

'Ed.' He replied.

'Well, first of all, I know what you, Ed, and Waller did to me.' Alex calmly said.

'How do you feel, I mean, Angry? But how have the Nanomachines been?' Clark struggled to hide his curiosity. His fear, vanished.

'As intended, I think. Headaches and blackouts, how do I stop them? They are becoming worse.'

'You had a calcified area of your brain. It didn't respond well whenever the compound tried to embed in and around it.' Clark said, looking at his head. 'So we tapered off the treatment, gave you less.'

'Can it be stopped?' Alex demanded, annoyed at how Clark studied him.

'Well. Dr Waller planned to use some targeted radiation. Burn the calcification away as such. Ed needed you out of the site. Someone had leaked information about what we were doing.' Clark said nervously.

'Listen, we don't have your family, we won't hurt them. I needed to speak to you that's all.' Alex explained. 'Can you help me stop the headaches?'

'Yes, yes, of course. It is not without risk I must say.' Clark held up his hands. 'It is a small area, a minor effort but the chance of Stroke or bleeding is a factor.'

'When?' Alex asked.

'I have a dinner meeting with the Dean for feedback and critical review of my presentation my calendar is clear from now.' Clark said excitedly. 'I have a private lab at my home. Follow me.'

Alex looked at Misha in the rear-view mirror. Her face concerned about some of what she had just witnessed.

They followed Clark for half an hour as he drove to a large, gated mansion. He punched in a code at the gate, and they tailgated him through and up the drive to the house.

'If anything goes wrong, he does anything to me that doesn't look right, anyone else shows up, shoot him, shoot them and get yourself as far away as possible.' Alex said as he squeezed Misha's hand. She nodded in reply.

A four-car garage annexed the house, it was converted into Clark's own lab. Several workstations spread across the room. Alex and Misha took it all in as Clark buzzed about writing down equations and testing what looked like a laser you would see removing a tattoo, but this was mounted on some sort of frame that could be adjust to any angle or height.

Alex could feel the aura increasing. He knew another attack was coming on. He grabbed Misha's arm. She knew straight away as his face drained of colour. The ringing in his ears made his eyes water. The pain in the side of his head. Like a stabbing blade that expanded the further it went in.

When he woke, he was sat semi recumbent in what reminded him of a dentist's chair. The ringing was gone. The pain was gone. He felt nauseated and a little shaky.

'How long this time?' He asked.

'An hour.' Misha's footsteps getting closer.

'Mr Brody, that was quite something.' Clark said from behind him. 'I think that it is time you both left. My family will return home soon and I keep them as far from my work as I can.'

'Are you gonna help me?' Alex sat up angry.

'I have. The lady will explain, I assume.' Clark pulled off a pair of blue nitrile gloves.

Misha drove the car out of Clark's long driveway to the gate. It was already opened. He was eager to have them gone before anyone would notice.

Alex felt exhausted. His eyelids could not be controlled, they closed against every attempt he made to stop them. He slept in the passenger seat until he felt Misha's hand in his pocket.

'Hey, it's okay, the cell phones, the hole, just leave it to me.' She whispered.

He wasn't sure how long it took her to hide them or how long it took to get back to the cabin. She helped him out the car, and inside.

'He said it could wipe you out for a day or two. Just relax. Do you need some water?' She asked.

She put down a bottle of water next to him as he lay on the couch. He could still feel the shaking, but it was internal, his hands were as still as a surgeons.

Misha stayed up most of the night, checking on him. He slept on and off. She placed a cold wet flannel across his brow as he burned up and cooled back down several times. She told herself, this is what Clark said would happen, she needed reassurance, she did not know what could come next. She spoke to him a few times. His speech was unchanged. Squeezed his hand. He squeezed back. She was glad he hadn't had a stroke, or worse.

He was easily rousable in the morning. He took on some fluids and managed to get himself to the bathroom. The light hurt his eyes. He felt nauseated. Misha placed a bucket next to where he lay. He still felt the inner trembling as his central nervous system tried to recuperate, adapt, something that he did not understand.

'We need some supplies. I'll check the cell phones when I pass.' She caressed his head as he lay, somewhere between sleep and a waking dream.

Misha took the Jeep. She had made a list of items they would need. She hoped Alex would be more himself by the time she got back. She pulled in where she had hidden the cell phones. When she dug them up she checked them both. The one from Truman. Nothing. The one from Manny had a missed call. No messages. She called Manny back.

'Hi Manny, this is Misha.' She said.

'Oh hey you. Where's Alex at?' Manny asked.

'He got the thing done to stop the headaches. He's pretty rough.'

'Oh man, you think you could come by? I have some more intel.' He could tell she was apprehensive with the pause. 'Won't take long, he needs to know sooner.' He played his hand, trying not to worry her.

'Yeah, will be a flying visit though, I need to get some things together.' She said.

Misha grabbed almost everything on her list from a gas station. She thought about calling Alex, telling him where she was going. She decided to let him rest. He would only worry. He didn't need that right now.

Misha pulled up outside Manny's place. Feeling anxious, it wrong being here without him. She felt she was overstepping a boundary. She rationalised that it would save them another trip tomorrow or the day after she thought. She could even get planning whilst Alex was still ropey.

She knocked on the door and Manny had pushed his remote for it to open.

'Misha baby, you good? My man Brody alright?' Manny smiled as he spoke.

'I'm fine, Alex is resting up. Are you alright?' Misha answered.

He nodded his head as he turned back to his monitor. 'Come see this girl.'

Misha walked over and looked at the screens. She couldn't understand much of what was going on, but it looked like financial records.

'So, I pulled these records and cross checked them they all go to the same person. Each person Alex has dealt with. From the Arc. Pays this one account.' Manny smiled, proud of his work.

'What do we do with this info?' Misha asked.

'The account gets accessed, same time, each week, at an ATM.' He said, rolling himself a joint.

'Where?' She said. 'When?'

'Duke's bar. Every single Tuesday.' Manny said, licking the glue strip along his rolling paper.

'I'll tell Alex when I get back.' Smiling. 'Thanks Manny, I don't know what he would do without you.'

Misha grabbed her jacket.

'You wanna stay for a bit, have a smoke, or a beer?' Manny asked.

'I really can't, I've already been gone too long. Hate driving in the dark.' She said, feeling awkward.

'Oh, yeah, no problem. Could you give this to Alex?' He held out a small pendant with the letter 'E' forming most of it. 'I found it where he collapsed the other night. Musta fell from his pocket. I recognised it as Emily's. Must be the last thing he has of her.'

'Oh of course, I'll make sure he gets it tonight.' Misha smiled taking the pendant. She hugged Manny and thanked him again on her way out. The smell of his smoke stuck to her hair, her least favourite thing about meeting Manny, the smoke.

As she drove back to the cabin. She felt bad for Manny. He was lonely. She wondered if she should have stayed a little longer, shared a beer or two. Talked about something that wasn't about the Arc of Evermore. She promised herself to give him more time, soon as Alex was better, they'd go eat out and have some drinks, make a night of it. She asked herself why she felt the need to lie about driving in the dark. She still had several hours of light left. There was something uneasy stirring inside of her.

She buried the phones at the usual spot and carried on up to the cabin. Nothing out of the ordinary. No new tracks. She knew she couldn't read the land like Alex but if a vehicle came through, she would know.

Alex heard the vehicle approaching, the diesel hum was his Jeep. It needed a tune up and carried an easily recognisable noise, when in the lower gear speeds. When Misha came in, he was still on the couch. His cell lay by him, an empty water bottle and his gun too. He wished he was up, ready, fresh and able for when she got back, there wasn't a chance, he was lucky to even have his eyes open.

'Hey, I picked up some supplies from a gas station. Should keep us fed and watered for a few days. How you feeling?' She asked as she started putting things in the fridge.

'Still a little tender, over the worst, I think.' Alex said, covering his eyes from the light.

'I checked the cell phones....' Misha said before Alex cut her off.

'Somebody's coming up the track.' He struggled to sit himself up. Every muscle burned as thought he had trained them for hours.

Misha pulled her gun and ran to the window. Alex noticed her posture change. She relaxed.

'It's Earl.' She said. 'Did you call him?'

'No.' Alex said.

Misha watched as Earl hauled himself out the minivan. He hobbled around to the sliding door on the side and pulled out a crate. It held several paper bags. Groceries, she wondered.

She opened the door and rushed to help him with the crate.

'Fuckin knees, do you know they only last about fifty years miss?' He laughed.

She carried the crate to the table and placed it down. Earl had negotiated the steps and entered the lounge. He set his eyes on Alex.

'You look like my bitch wife did when she was getting eaten inside out by the cancer.' Earl stood over him, considering his words. 'Joel, son, you ain't fuckin dyin are you?'

'No, Earl, I'm not dying' Alex answered, putting on an act to get himself sat up without feeling sick.

'Good, cos that's extra rent I'll need. Triple if I have to bury you round back.' Earl slapped his thigh as he laughed at himself. 'Well, I figured you folks would need some supplies up here, I brought some food and more bourbon.'

'Earl that's so sweet of you.' Misha thanked him.

'Well, thing is, you'll need to share the bourbon.' He winked, laughing. 'Joel, you get some radiation in you? You remind me of the state my wife was in after she got it.'

'Yeah, targeted treatment, guaranteed to make me useless for a few days.' Alex said.

Earl nodded his head, poured a bourbon and hobbled outside. Alex and Misha exchanged a glance, shared a smile. They could hear Earl talking to himself.

'Fixed that roof real good, son, I can evict you now.' Earl shouted from outside. Laughing to himself.

Alex thought about having a bourbon with Misha and Earl, but the thought made him even more nauseated. Earl shared stories of his wife, calling her the bitch, laughing, making them laugh. He pulled some photos from his time in Vietnam with the Army, he was always a wiry, thin man.

Earl was stood by the window as Alex retuned from another failed attempt to empty his stomach. He hung his photos back on the nail that stuck out of the timber.

'You folks got some family coming?' Earl asked.

'No, you are our only visitor, why?' Alex said.

'Two damn SUV's coming up the track, that's why.' Earl turned to face them.

'Earl, you'd better get going, they are here for me.' Alex said.

Earl limped over to the cabinet and unlocked it.

'These limp dick fuckers are on my land.' Earl grabbed his lever action Winchester out, checked it was still loaded and looked over at Misha. 'Can you shoot, missy?'

She nodded and Earl threw her the shotgun. She checked it and looked at Alex.

'Misha, the plan, go out the back and get as far as you can.' He looked out the window. Two vehicles outside. Each had it's 4 doors open. He counted eight men, armed.

She went to him and kissed him. He grabbed her arm and she winced.

'Sorry.' He said.

'No, no, it's this.' She replied, pulling out the pendant Manny had passed her. She had stuffed it in her arm splint.

He took it in his hand. 'What is this?' His face showed his surprise.

'Manny said it was Emily's.' She said. A question forming on her lips before she decided not to continue.

For a moment, Alex froze where he stood.

A voice boomed from outside the cabin.

'We are only here for the Nothingman. Nobody else needs to get hurt. You have the word of the Arc of Evermore!'

Alex urged Misha to go, she left via the back door. He looked at Earl.

'You don't need to get hurt Earl, I'll go out and surrender.' Alex said.

'The hell you will, son, these pussies can fuck off!' Earl barked.

The sound of glass shattering and the crack from the shot that was fired filled the cabin. Alex ducked. Earl just stood. The voice shouted again.

'That was one of a couple hundred bullets that will pepper that shithole if you don't come out!' The unknown man bellowed.

Earl limped to the door and swung it open. Alex watched through a crack in the blinds as he saw all eight men raise their guns. The leader, who had done all the shouting spoke quietly to them. They lowered their weapons. A mix of carbine rifles and shotguns, Alex noticed.

The man slowly, arrogantly walked towards Earl, laughing to himself.

'You ain't The Nothingman, where is he?' He asked.

'Get off my fuckin land.' Earl barked.

'Listen you old ....' Earl cut the man off.

'I didn't serve two tours of Viet-fuckin-nam for some pansy and his group of slack jawed shit kickers to come on up talking to me on my land like I'm the asshole!'

The man pulled a face and before he could even understand what Earl had said to him. Earl raised the rifle to his chest and blasted him off the top step. The shot echoed through the forest and the cabin in full stereo. Earl had already flicked the lever and started raining down more shots to the men ducking behind the SUV's. One of them caught a round in the neck and dragged himself underneath one of the cars.

Alex ducked as automatic fire ripped through the cabin. He watched on as Earl limped back inside and shut the door as glass, splintered wood and dust took to the air all around him.

He shouted at Earl. 'Get down.'

'Not in my own home' His eyes darting from Alex to the window. 'Now fucking shoot somebody!' Earl laughed.

Alex let off some rounds from his Glock through the window. He was sure he had hit at least two men as they tried to flank the cabin. Earl pulled up a section of floorboard as Alex tried to work out the attacker's plan. When Alex turned to warn Earl of the men moving closer Earl was stood with a hand grenade.

'I'm gonna need your arm for this, son.' Earl said before rolling the grenade along the floor to Alex.

Alex pulled the pin and threw it out the window to where three of the men had mistakenly stayed too close together. A loud bang. The blinds swung in showering what remained of the windowpane on top of him. The concussion rattled the air, stronger than he remembered. He peeked from his cover and saw two men, unmoving, laying maimed by the shrapnel.

Everything was quiet. Alex reloaded his gun. Earl had sat himself in a chair as he pushed more rounds into the Winchester.

'How many left?' Earl asked, too relaxed for what was happening.

'I can't tell. Maybe 5 down.' Alex said. Noting that it was far too quiet.

Another barrage of shots ripped through the cabin. He noticed from the corner of his eye that Earl had recoiled in the chair.

'Earl! Are you hit?' He shouted.

'Yep. It's a kill. In my chest.' He gargled a little whilst he got the words out.

A subtle creak on the floor was followed by the handle of the door turning slowly. A loud crack rang out. The Winchester blasted off another shot through the front door. A loud thud and the noise a man makes in his death rattle could be heard from outside.

Alex crawled over to Earl. He had dropped the rifle.

'I get to go be with my bitch wife now, son. I miss her.' Earl fought to get the words out.

Alex helped him to the floor, where he took his last breath.

Alex knew a man stood behind him. He had heard him as soon as he crossed from the back deck onto the tiled kitchen floor. He was not prepared for what came next. A sharp stab in his mid-back. Then the spasms. The bastard has tasered me, he thought.

He was fully aware of what they did to him in between taser blasts. The cable ties dug into his skin. Even as he lay still. The nausea was made worse by the many thousand volts that on the last blast, was the sixth.

He smelled a mixture of breath mint and cologne. Somebody moved closer to him.

'Well. You are my million dollars asshole. Try anything, you get a shock. Speak, you get a shock. Get it?' The man whispered, trying to make himself seem scary. Professional.

Alex never answered. Never moved. Either two more men arrived or two that he thought were hurt, weren't. They manhandled him into the trunk of one of the vehicles. A pillowcase over the head prevented him seeing which one.

'He been searched?' The man's voice again. 'Why you shaking your head, Dan. Does that mean no?'

He felt hands checking his, legs, groin and pockets.

'The hell is this?' The pillowcase was violently pulled from his head.

'This mean something to you?' The man said.

Alex nodded his head as he thought the face matched the voice. A little big man. Trying too hard to be mean. To be the man. He was re-hooded. The pendant shoved back into his pocket. The trunk slammed shut and he felt as though they were in reverse. That would make sense, he rationalised. Nowhere to turn with the minivan and Jeep sitting. Misha, he thought about how far she ran. If they caught her. Was she in the other SUV?

He was dragged from the trunk sometime after. It was dark. Then up a few stairs. He noticed a change in the surface his feet touched. Dirt, concrete, then carpet.

Chapter 18

The shooting started, stopped, and started again by the time she crouched behind a fallen tree. An even louder bang. Wait, she thought. She knew what the plan was, but she knew what she wanted to do. Alex wasn't in a fit state to fight this one out. She heard the grumble of the vehicles leaving. Slowly. As she got closer, she heard the whine of the reverse gear when it's driven faster than a crawl. Outside the cabin, she paused, listening. She heard nothing but the blinds rustle in the wind through the broken windows. Inside, it was dark, she used it to her advantage. The dark form of a body lay next to the table. She could tell it was Earl. His thin frame easily distinguishable. A pool of blood under his torso. She looked at him, sadness filling her thoughts.

There was no one else around. Alex's gun lay on the floor next to his knife. Drag marks with streaks of blood were visible on the porch, in front of the house, and by the side. His burner still lay next to the couch. Palpitations in her chest. She knew they had him. Wondering if he was hurt, where they might take him. She dropped a blanket over Earl's body, grabbed the rifle and shotgun, and jumped into the Jeep.

She retrieved the hidden cell phones and called Manny, she was in a frenzy.

'Manny, they have got Alex!' Shouting, voice weakening. 'I don't know where they have taken him.'

'Was he hurt?' Manny asked.

'I. I have no idea. There was a gunfight. His things, the gun, his knife. All laid out on the floor.' Misha fought the lump in her throat to get her words out.

'Where are you? Can you get to me, safely?' He said trying to ground her.

'Yeah. Yeah. Fuck. I'm already heading your way.' She breathed heavily as she spoke.

Misha had to add some calm to her driving. She did not need to be pulled over by the law. This was the first time she had lost her cool. Felt out of control. Since her first assignment to a VIP. Her mind drifted to that day. A wealthy Israeli arms dealer thought she was too pretty to be his stateside bodyguard. His eyes undressed her at every opportunity. She distanced herself and only communicated with official language, no flirting, no friendliness. He had tried to force himself on her in his hotel room as she ran a sweep. She managed to break free from his grasp, before he managed to sexually assault her. She remembered how hard she had hit him with the champagne bottle. She thought she had killed him. She vowed to never feel as vulnerable as she did that day, ever again. Her employed reprimanded and reduced her pay for the subsequent assignments due to being out of control. Misha knew she would get over it back then, she wasn't so sure she would get over this if anything happened to Alex.

As the Jeep came to a halt outside Manny's, she realised that she had very little recollection of the journey. She removed her arm splint in the car, checked her sidearm, and stuffed Alex's knife into her pocket.

As she walked into Manny's lounge, she noticed a pair of half packed bags on the sofa. Toiletries and other products sat in a clear bag as if waiting to be packed away. A steampunk style clock, made from old bulbs and plumbing pipe told her it was not long after midnight.

'I've pinged the cell I gave him several times. Seems it lags for hours. Over by Maple Forest. Couple clicks out.' Manny said.

'He doesn't have it.' Head in her hands, she spoke.

'Right. So, who took him? Truman?' He asked.

'No. They identified themselves as The Arc.' She stood shaking her head. 'You are leaving?'

'My sister, visiting her down in New Orleans. Haven't seen her since her boy was born.' Manny typed furiously as he explained. 'I'll delay. We need to find Alex. Before they do something to him.'

'How are you going to find him, we have nothing to go on?' Misha asked.

'These folk can't shut up. They are always chattin shit on the dark web. It'll take a minute, though.' Manny replied, immersed in the scrolls of text facing him.

Misha paced the room. She felt useless. Five times, she counted, the number of times she checked her gun. Her eyes bored into Manny as he worked all six screens, his fingers tap dancing along the keyboard, sweeping his cursor in all directions. She knew he knew she watched on, impatiently.

Chapter 19

Alex felt his backside go numb from the hard chair he was bound to. He had no idea how long he had been in this place. Hours. Not days. He could manoeuvre enough to get the pillowcase off his head, he chose to allow these men to feel in complete control. He never spoke. Several men came and went. He could feel the presence of one man. Not too far from him. He occasionally shifted where he sat. He breathed quietly but Alex was aware that he never left the room. There were times that the footsteps were quietened, muffled, by the carpet. Sometimes there was a change in the footsteps. Three clear steps then pacing, a hollower sound to the stepping. The sounds changed in front of him. He assumed the room they held him had two levels, or a mezzanine.

Alex started to think about how he was going to get out from his restraints. The chair had no give, it was solid. He had seen movies; desperate men try to collapse a chair to serve as the stimulus for an elaborate escape. In truth, he knew first hand that the likelihood of success was almost zero. First, he was being observed, second, the cable ties were thick and tight to the skin, lastly, he had a feeling that the little man would make a mistake.

Footsteps, again. A clunk, something dropped to the ground. A bag, maybe, he considered.

Tap. Tap. Tap. Tap. He heard.

'Did he fall or was he pushed? A voice asked from in front. 'How much momentum is required to cave in a man's skull?' It asked, more left than dead ahead. It wasn't the man who had taken him from the cabin. This new player had an heir of superiority. It was in his voice.

The hood was ripped from his head. There you are Alex thought, knowing it was his adversary from the cabin. He was stood behind Alex, he smelled the cologne, he knew it was him. Dead ahead, was a podium with a lectern, slightly to the left, a few metres away was a thick timber column, floor to ceiling. He knew he was at Walker-Mills. An older man stood by the column. There you are, oh important one, Alex thought. It was not Harvey Jupiter. He checked himself for being too optimistic.

'Nothingman.' The man said, disgust in his voice. 'Did my brother truly fall from the podium?' He moved closer. Bushy black eyebrows. Slicked back white hair. A Large hooked nose. Alex could see the similarity, if they were in fact biological brothers, and not in some cult sense. 'Did you enjoy smashing his head against an immovable object? Is this what satisfies you? Do you feel that you can justify your actions when you are held to task?'

Alex sat in silence. It came sooner than he expected. A thud that sent his head to the left. A stinging throbbing pain across his right ear.

'The deacon is talking to you.' Angry little man spat as he shouted. 'Fucking show some respect!'

The old man spoke up. 'Carson, hands off! Prepare your equipment. The Nothingman will tell us what we require.'

'Yes, Deacon Shanks.' Carson spoke like a scolded child.

The old man stood close enough that he could have struck Alex himself. He unbuttoned his peacoat, slowly, deliberately. Focusing on every movement with precision and repetition.

He folded his coat like it was a rare historical relic going into a display case. Shanks placed it upon the podium. The noise of metal clinking continued behind Alex. Torture, he assumed.

'Carson. Bind his hands, where they will be seen.' Shanks spoke, as he dressed himself in an apron. One that would look at home on a butcher.

'Hard way or easy?' Carson moved himself into Alex's field of vision. Taser in is hand.

Alex didn't speak.

'Our problem will take the easy way Carson. Now do what I have requested!' The voice of Shanks bellowed.

Carson cut the Ziplock ties that held his hands to the chair back. Alex flexed and extended his wrists to get some blood flow back. Before he was told or manhandled, he placed his forearms and hands along the armrests. He could feel the fear from Carson as he got close to him. His breathing faster. Body language, poised, ready to withdraw or run. Alex allowed him to Ziplock each wrist to the armrest.

The Deacon stood ahead of Alex. He made far too much effort to pull the long cuff medical gloves on. Alex had interrogated men before. He knew these tactics rarely made much difference. All theatre, he thought.

'Nothingman.' Deacon Shanks leaned in. 'Do you know how much trouble you have caused us? You are a man without limits. A man with nothing to lose, they say.' He held out a hand to the side, eyes staring into Alex's. 'I will do things to you that will make you wish for death.' Carson handed him a nail gun. 'Then I will give you death.'

The Deacon placed the nail gun against the back of Alex's right hand. He grabbed his chin and pulled his head up. He held eye contact with Alex as he pulled the trigger.

The sound of expelled air from Alex's nose as he gritted his teeth was all that was heard in the room. The burning. The heat from the transfer of kinetic energy played on every single pain receptor in his hand. He managed not to scream.

'Who do you work for. Who provides the information and orders for you to attack The Arc of Evermore?' Shanks spat as he asked him.

Alex offered nothing. He just looked at him. The pain in his hand becoming worse. The throbbing was intense.

'You have made an inconvenient intervention to our progress. Are you a liberal just doing his job? The deacon spoke. He handed the nail gun back to Carson and gave him a nod. 'Our modus operandi is one you could find quite noble if you care to consider rather than destroy.'

Carson entered his field of vision again. The Deacon held up two fingers to him, he smiled in reply. Alex stared at Carson as he approached him, a pair of pliers in hand. First, he took the fingernail from the pinky finger. It was quick. The stinging sensation extended to something higher up in the arm. Alex gritted his teeth. His eyes watered and he began to feel nauseated. This, clearly irritated Carson. He placed the mouth of the pliers over the end of the next finger. This time, he pulled slowly, applying a slight rotation to tear the nailbed in sections. Alex let out a scream that made Carson recoil, taking the rest of the nail off. Carson laughed as droplets of Alex's blood ran down to the floor.

'Now I believe I have your attention.' Shanks stood hands clasped at his chest in a faux prayer position. 'Women are made for suffering. We will use them to give us children. Pleasure. Solace, even, if they are worthy. The part most philistines object to is the children.' He retrieved a bag of medical blood from the podium and held it as he spoke. 'The blood of the pure, the young, feeds the needy, nourishes the enlightened. It is the difference between you and I. Evermore is in my reach, you will be nothing more than hog feed.'

Alex had maintained composure as the Deacon spoke. The pain, excruciating, ever present, lapped up his arm in waves, pulsing with fervour.

'Now, Nothingman, tell me who you work for. Is it the U.S Government?' The Deacon stood, studying Alex for any betrayal in his eyes.

'No.' Alex grinned as he said it.

Not accustomed to that type of response, the Deacon flew into a fit of rage. He slapped Alex across the face with his gloved hand. 'You cannot influence this! You cannot change it! You will die! That is the only thing that is written, here!' He closed his eyes, breathing deeply. 'Carson, make this subhuman animal wish for his death. I will return in ten minutes.'

Alex took a deep breath. He watched the Deacon leave from the door at the rear of the podium. Carson stood facing Alex. 'Tell us who sent you and I promise I'll just shoot you, if you don't, the Deacon's next move is to find your family and hurt them in front of you. If you have a daughter some of the guys will fuck her, as you watch.' He laughed as he stretched off his neck, readying himself.

Alex felt the rage simmering inside. He promised himself that Carson would beg him for mercy before he killed him. He thought for a second, they really do not know who I am, what they already did to my family.

His head jerked to the left after the first punch. Then, the second. The taste of blood filled the inside of his mouth. Only noises, at first, then the dull pain creeping in. Carson pounded him to the left side of his face several times. Flashes, dull noises with every hit. He had been hit harder but he wasn't sure how much he could take before he became unconscious. Throbbing around his left eye, a narrowing field of vision, he would be lucky to be able to see from it soon he thought. Carson had delivered some solid punches to his abdomen. He fought for air as his Diaphragm spasmed. A rush of cold saliva in his mouth. He vomited as Carson leaned in for another body shot. It sprayed his face and chest.

'Arrrghhh, what the fuck?!' He screamed as he wiped his face using his hands. 'I'm going to enjoy cutting your throat after that you piece of shit.'

Alex let out a laugh that betrayed the way he currently looked. A fine trickle of blood from above his left eye, almost swollen shut. His beard shiny with semi clotted blood from his nose down to his chin.

Carson had grabbed a meat cleaver as he laughed. It caught the light as he raised it up by his waist. Before he had any chance to swing it the Deacon called out. 'Carson, stand down!'

'Yes Deacon.' Like a scolded child once again, Carson placed the weapon down and stepped back from Alex.

'I will allow him to remove your skin next.' Shanks smiled, falsely. 'I have located your family Nothingman.' He studied Alex intensely as those words were spoken. 'They will be here within the hour. I will take the youngest and remove their entire volume of blood before transfusing it into you.' He removed what looked like an IV kit from a bag behind. Ensuring Alex saw it when he placed it, slowly, deliberately at the podium. 'You will watch as we use your wife to sow the next seed, the next blood sacrifice will be all because of you.'

'You alrcady have.' Alex finally spoke. The look on the face of the Deacon and Carson intrigued Alex at that moment. '33rd street, car bombing. That was my wife and daughter.'

The Deacon and Carson exchanged a glance that confused Alex. He couldn't quite place what he had saw. Footsteps. The doorway behind Alex. Someone else was coming. 'Deacon Shanks, Mr Carson, the Nothingman's wife is here.' A man's voice announced. Both smiled. Thwack! Carson punched Alex square in the face as they both walked past him. His head recoiled backwards, and the chair followed. He lay on his back, still bound to the chair as he watched the figures disappear into the corridor.

Chapter 20

Click. Click. Click. The bird pecked against the glass as spiderweb cracks appeared all around. She woke with a start. She sat on Manny's couch. Shit. She thought, must have fallen asleep. Click. Click. Click. It was Manny's fingers dancing along the keyboard.

'I think I know where they took our boy!' Manny spoke as he wheeled himself to face her.

'Okay, where?' She stood up too quickly, she had to give herself a second as she wobbled, a kaleidoscope like haze dancing across her eyes.

'Could be two places. Lotta goons chatting about the docks but, I'm seeing a few messages go out on the dark web. Manny rubbed his hands together, excitedly or needing another joint, she could not tell which. 'The farm he hit, it's in code but I'm seeing this.' He pointed to the screen. A post from someone called ArcUnlimited12, it read;

Nothing like a blood offer **man** got him. Walker-Mills.

'They are gonna kill him.' Manny said. 'I've seen this shit before, they are all about spilling blood. Re seeding the earth with blood, using blood to reach Evermore man. It's proper creepy.'

Misha grabbed her things. Stuffed her handgun into her waistband she spoke to Manny. 'I can't let this happen. I need to go Manny, thank you.'

Manny reached out and grabbed her wrist. 'You can't seriously be thinkin you can go there and get him?'

'I don't have a choice, Manny!' Misha said, knowing the task she faced was unsurmountable.

'If I wasn't in this fuckin chair..... I .....' He looked down at his legs as he said the words.

Misha placed her hand on his, still holding her wrist. 'You have done more than enough, he knows it, I'll make sure he knows how much.' She kissed him on the top of his dreadlocks and left.

The nausea. The dry mouth. The sound of her own heart beating. Misha could barely hear the motor start-up as she turned the key. She dragged the shotgun into the passenger seat from where it was laying in the back. She used Alex's cell phone to retrieve the details of the Walker-Mills farm and refreshed herself with the route.

The sun had decided it was time to nourish the land as she drove. It was early morning. It hung low, casting a beautiful orange glow across the land. Fighting her own thoughts, she meandered around the possibility that Alex was already dead. She remembered the gate. The idea of ramming through it came first. The armed guard would raise the alarm or shoot her on approach. She shook her head and cast that idea out. The way she and Alex accessed the place a few days prior, that had to be the way, she thought. Dump the car, go in quiet, on foot.

She recognised the rolling hills, the sun casting finger like shadowed striations over them. The beautiful forests that lined the road in between roads leading to working ranches and farms. Acutely aware of her breathing becoming faster, she turned on the radio, hoping to break her overpowering thoughts. A church bell clanged several times, a heavy metal guitar let out some blasts. For whom the bell tolls, a song by

Metallica played. The irony was not lost on her. She switched the radio off again.

The Jeep passed by the entrance to Walker-Mills farm. The gate, closed, the guard, sat in his sentry box. She parked in a rest area within a mile of the service road they had used before. She breeched the shotgun, emptying its ammunition and reloaded it. She chambered a round and removed the magazine from her handgun. She pushed an extra round into the magazine to replace the one that was in the chamber. Flicking the small switches, she made sure each weapon had the safety off. She was sat with one of Alex's cell phones in her hand as glass from the driver side window rained all over her. A hand reached in and grabbed her with the hair. She reached out and tried to grab her gun from the passenger seat. Too far. The hand yanked and pulled at her. Her head was half out the window as her attacker realised the seatbelt was still around her. A flash in her eyes. A muffled thud. She felt the punch then as a little bit of fight went out of her. Same side that bore Truman's backhand. They must have cut the belt as she was dragged through the window where the man let her go. She was almost into the press up position to get herself up when he kicked her in the face.

They tossed her limp body across the backseats of a pickup and drove back towards Walker-Mills. Her eyes closed, she could hear them talking and laughing as they drove. Her face was in agony. She could tell her lip was split when she ran her tongue along the inside. Her cheekbone was throbbing. It took everything she had to avoid holding her face after the kick. She thought they'd stop if she feigned being knocked out cold. The vehicle stopped. Her heart beat out of her chest. She thought about what was next, does she try fight her way out the car or wait. The door opened next to her head. An unknown voice spoke. 'Oh, yeah. They'll be interested. Go on up, I'll call it in.'

The door slammed shut and they were moving again. She heard the two men in front talk about her body and their intentions. When the vehicle came to a stop again, she decided to lay still. The door opened and they dragged her out. Her wrists ached with the man's grasp, her not fully healed fracture directly under his hand, and she must have twitched or tensed a muscle as he quickly grabbed her by the throat. He shouted. 'Even a little bit of fight, I'll crush it. Relax!'

They threw her onto something solid. A table she thought. She looked up and saw white streaks of cloud scar the blue sky. They were outside. She tried to roll but was held by two men. Again, one had her throat in his grasp. She felt someone else hold her legs. They bound her to whatever she lay on. It was tight. No movement. She braced herself as they dragged it a few metres. Her view of the sky slowly changed to a view of the Ranch, the grounds and 4 men standing, looking at her. They had upended the table.

She watched as a man wearing what looked like a butcher's apron walked to her. 'Well. I can hurt the Nothingman some more before I kill him. Thank you, for that pleasure.' He smiled a sick smile as he stared into her eyes.

Chapter 21

Alex stared at the ceiling light as he lay there. His view becoming obscured with the face of Carson. He was helped by another to lift Alex upright. Alex noticed he had snips in his hand. Wondered if it was to take his fingers.

'Tough guy. I'll tell you what's gonna happen.' Carson, chest puffed out spoke. 'I cut you free. You walk out to where we have your wife.'

'My wife is dead Carson. You heard that part, right?' Alex said.

'Well. Who's the hot piece of ass driving your fucking Wrangler?' Carson smiled.

Misha, Alex thought. How, could she have known where they took him? He asked himself.

His ties we snipped. He realised how much pain he was in as he stood up. His body screaming out. A nudge to turn. Another to start walking. Against his back, it was cold. Gun or taser, he wondered. He started thinking how to systematically take them out. The next touch, he thought. He backed himself to at least kill one, but not if he got a shot off. He needed to see who they had outside. He walked and did as his captors asked.

He noticed the orange glow of the sun dominate the land outside. Early morning. The smell of the air. The morning due, dusting the grass and bushes. Then he saw several men standing around someone. The outline of Deacon Shanks the only he knew. He was heading towards them. That was when he saw her. Tied to something that stood her up. Misha. He felt a strange combination of being glad to see her and deep concern.

138

Another nudge in his back, no effect. He stood his ground. Misha was about 40 strides from him. The tree line maybe 100. Two men behind him. The deacon, midway between him and Misha. Carson walked toward another two men standing nearby Misha.

'This is where I offer you a choice.' Shanks stood. A dominating presence to his men. A figure of seniority. 'Tell me who you work for. I bring you death quickly.' He continued. 'Option two, I allow the men to have your wife over here, as you watch. I skin you, then kill you.'

'What part did you not get? Your attack on 33rd killed everything I had. I'm here to make sure that never happens to another person.' Alex shook his head. Appalled at what these people claimed was their right. Their beliefs.

'This, with the 33rd street thing again. Shanks shouted. 'Who is this woman? CIA, FBI?'

'No, she's with me. You shouldn't have touched her.' His eyes burning a hole in the Deacon.

The Deacon could see something in Alex's eyes, it terrified him, but he knew showing a weakness would end badly. 'Oh, well you won't like what happens now you have not answered my question. Shanks laughed, unconvincingly. 'Carson!'

He felt the taser pressed into the small of his back. Each arm hooked by the two goons who were behind him. Carson grabbed at Misha. Tearing at her belt and buttons. She squirmed around as much as she could to make it harder for him. He hit her in the stomach and had ripped her jeans down to her knees, exposing her underwear. He held her by the throat with one hand. His face decorated in a sick expression as he gritted his teeth. The other hand pulled at her, trying to remove her underwear.

Tap. Tap. Tap. Something metal. He followed it with his eyes into the nearby treeline. He recognised it as the one he had used to access the farm. He saw the muzzle flash. He was awakened. His senses firing on all cylinders. A reddish mist exploded from the side of Carson's head. He dropped to the ground, like someone hit an off switch, it was over for him. The gunshot rang out in the vast countryside. Another muzzle flash. Two more quick gunshots. The other men drop to the dirt. The two men still grasp at his arms. Taser at his back. The Deacon begins to break into a quickened stride towards the building.

'Hey old fucker! Stop!' A familiar voice. Alex thought. His eyes fixed on Misha. Another shot. This time closer to Alex. It missed everyone. Deacon shanks stood still; it had the desired effect.

Alex turned back towards the treeline. Aided by his new friends. Human shield. Alex was shocked as he saw the stocky outline of a man striding towards them working the lever action of a Winchester and raising it back up to eye level as he moved closer.

The breaths of the men holding him were now at a rapid rate. The gun pointed at them, or Alex himself. He couldn't possibly tell.

'Let him go you fucking freaks!' It was loud, his voice bouncing back from the building.

'It's a taser. Shoot them!' Alex said with a laugh. He closed his eyes.

The warm spray of blood he felt on his ear precluded the noise and change in air pressure. His right knee buckled as the man's body fell against it. His left arm, free from grasp. Alex opened his eyes turning to his left, just in time to see the man getting shot in the neck as he ran away. He turned as Ed Truman had thrown the Winchester to the ground, pulling a Colt .45 from a shoulder holster. A gun lay at his own feet. It wasn't a taser.

Deacon Shanks held his hands out as Truman approached. 'Now. Spare me and I will see you rewarded, financially of course!'

Alex sprinted to Misha. 'Hey, hey, are you okay, let me get you off this.' He pulled her jeans back up and untied the ligatures on her wrists and ankles. He held her tight.

'Tell this man what he wants to know. He asks, you fucking answer. I'll ensure you get back to your business.' Truman stood pushing the pistol into the cheekbone of Shanks.

Misha nodded at Alex. He walked back to where the Deacon and Truman both stood. 'Okay, Nothingman. Ask this sick fuck what you need to!' Truman sniffed. Alex wondered if it was an upper airway issue or Cocaine.

'Who do you report to? Where is Harvey Jupiter?' Alex demanded.

'My superior is untouchable. I don't know where Mr Jupiter is. Nobody knows except his security detail.' The Deacon shook as he spoke.

'What is at Duke's bar? Alex raised his voice. His face hurting.

'A safe zone. It's a pickup and drop off site. Our contacts in public office prefer a discreet place. We own the bar. Can control it.' The Deacon adjusted the apron he still wore.

Before anyone could speak again, Truman turned to Alex asking. 'What's with the apron? He about to butcher you?' Truman over acted that he was shocked before speaking again. 'I was gonna wait till he had the sirloin off you. But, you know, the midget.' Jutting his chin towards the corpse of Carson. 'Misha is off limits, remember.'

'Now. If you'll be done.' The deacon using his palms to gesture he was done. 'I will make sure you are well compensated.'

Bang.

Truman shot him in face at point blank range. The Deacon dropped on the spot. A plume of smoke coming from the hole in his cheek. His body twitched as Truman kicked him several times.

'The fuck are you doing with a Winchester in your car?' Truman laughed as he walked back into the treeline. 'C'mon it's time to go.' He tossed a dressing to Alex. He wrapped his hand as they walked, a grimace adorned on his face as he balled his fist to hold the dressing in place.

Truman was quiet for the whole of the walk into the forest and down the service road. Alex checked on Misha as they walked. She assured him that she was. If Truman wasn't present, he would check her physically, tell her how happy he was that she was alive, how happy he was to see her. He was sure she would do the same.

Truman's car sat at the end of the service road.

'I'll take you to your Jeep. You need a new window.' Truman got in and started the engine. 'We have things to discuss. Follow me to the hangar.'

Truman stopped alongside Alex's car. They got out and he sat until Alex's car started and he was ready. The cascading beauty of the trees, hills, and their colours all but a blur as they tailed Truman.

'How did you find me? His hand assessing her wounds. Not wanting to take his eyes off the road too long. He noticed the split lip. The swelling to her cheekbone and a few small cuts on her forehead and left cheek.

Her eyes were fixated on him. She saw the bruising. Dried blood. Laceration over his eye. The swelling. 'I'm sorry I didn't get their faster! It took Manny a while to find out where you were taken.'

'How did he find me? I had no cell phone.' He asked.

'People chatting, the dark web.' Misha replied, she looked at his hand. Two fingernails missing. Hand bandaged primitively. Blood seeping through at the centre of his palm. 'My god, Alex, what did they do?'

'Nail gun. Pliers.' He answered. Confused. Misha. Manny. Truman. All circling in his thoughts. He winced. Sneezed and his eyes watered as she used wet wipes to clean the blood from his face. He saw in his peripheral vision as she used the mirror in the sun visor to check her own injuries.

'I text S.O.S to Truman from your phone.' Misha pointed at the phone. 'I didn't know what else to do. Manny was packed to go to his sister's. If I hadn't got there in time. Truman must have tracked the cell.'

'You sure Manny said sister?' He asked.

'Yeah, something about New Orleans.' She looked at him, confused.

'Manny doesn't have a sister.' Alex said.

They pulled in to Jackton airfield and followed the road to where the hangar stood. Alex was conflicted. Anger and confusion dominating his thoughts. He ran scenarios in his head. Most, if not all were bad. Misha sat confused. Feeling as though it was wrong to ask Truman for help. She didn't understand the current situation, or how it had formulated, she was about to be raped, tied to a table less than an hour ago. The shooting. Manny. Her headache, exacerbated as she churned the events around and around her head.

He struggled to conceal his agony when he got out the car. Misha noticed. He took a breath and walked into the hangar. Truman waved them into the office on the ground floor. It was brightly lit. Various documents littered the table. A few workplace safe posters spread across the walls. Advocating the use of high visibility clothing and such. Truman sat in a leatherback chair, he gestured for them to sit on the other seats. They sat. Alex, with difficulty.

'You owe her your life.' Truman said first. He cut the end from a cigar. 'I tracked that fucking phone to your car. Put two and two together with that fucking farm you already hit. That's the first time I've shot a Winchester.' He lit his cigar and laughed.

Alex looked at him in the eye. He decided to test him. 'Ed, I owe you some thanks. But I'm not sure it's for saving us back there or for allowing them to track us to the cabin.' Alex simmered with anger. 'Have you been telling them where I am?' He winced as he sat forward. 'You been trying to test your newest attack dog?'

'Ok. You have had your strike kid. I just shot 6 people, like a fucking Clint Eastwood western. Those people had hurt you. Probably gonna kill you.' He took a long pull on his cigar. 'First time I tracked that thing was today. I haven't always told you the truth but listen to my words.' He sniffed and continued. 'You are an asset to me. More useful alive than dead.' He stood up with his hand outstretched. 'Give them to me, the cells.'

They passed their cell phoned to Truman. He flipped open a laptop and plugged them into it. One of Truman's operators entered the room. He handed bottled water to Alex and Misha. Truman typed for a few seconds and spoke. 'This one, my issue, one tracking hit.' He turned it to show them. 'This one, Misha's, no tracking hits.' Reaching for the third phone. 'This one, pinged multiple times over the last couple of days. Its got a labyrinth of encryption. Can't say where you have been tracked from.'

Misha looked at Alex, assessing his face. 'Do you have a bug sweeper here?' He asked Truman.

Truman, looked interested 'No. Why?'

Alex reached inside his pocket and removed the pendant he took from Misha at the cabin. 'This.' He tossed it to Truman. He caught it in one hand.

They both watched on as Truman placed it on the table before using his Colt to smash it. He started laughing as he held up a tiny pill shaped object before the light. 'I think you have your answer.' Truman tossed it back to Alex.

'Shit, Alex, I didn't...' Mouth caught open, Misha sat, frozen.

'He used you, Misha. You are not responsible for this.'

Truman cut in 'I suggest you deal with your shit Brody. Take a few days to heal.' He stubbed out his cigar. 'I will be in touch.' He walked out the room.

Alex used the bathroom before they left. He dropped the tracker down the sink after he washed his face. The water spinning, tinged red with his blood, made its way down behind the tiny metal device. Good luck keeping track of that, he thought. Misha stood at the door of the hangar. She rotated her hand, testing out her previously injured arm. He thought about the rage he felt as Carson clawed at her, trying to do the unthinkable. He thought about the odds of Truman making that shot and decided not to go down that route, thinking of another loss, had he missed. An important question answered, he thought, the others would have to wait.

'Where should we go? I'll drive, you get some rest.' Misha spoke as she held his chin and looked his face over, studying the damage.

'I think we can almost trust Truman after that.' Alex breathed deeply. 'Let's go see old Clarence again.'

They travelled the short journey to the Silent Knight Motel. The wind forced its way through the Jeep's broken driver's window, unrelenting at any speed over 40kph. Several cars were parked up. An elderly woman sat in a deck chair smoking.

Clarence looked up from a newspaper as the door chime chirped. His face, a clear reflection of his thoughts as he laid his eyes on Misha.

'Oh, it's none of my business but, are you okay Ms. Gray?' Genuine concern tinted with a lustful sweep of his eyes to her body. 'Do you need a room?'

'Clarence. Hi. Please, a room for tonight.' She subconsciously ran her hands over her waist, checking that her jeans were buttoned, she knew the zip was burst and torn by Carson.

'Will it be just you or is...' Clarence stopped. Looking past Misha as Alex walked in behind her. 'Mr. Gray, it looks like you may need a doctor, I mean, it's not my business.' He petered off. Maybe it was the look on Alex's face.

'Clarence, thank you for your concern.' He walked over to the desk. 'It's amazing how banged up you can get in a car accident.' He smiled, placing a fifty dollar note on the table before Clarence. 'I trust that will cover this evening?'

'Of course, Mr Gray, I no longer have room 3, will number 9 be adequate?' Clarence, spoke as he slowly retracted his palm that covered the cash toward him.

'Yes.' Alex held his hand out for the key card.

They grabbed what little they had from the car. Alex pulled his .38 snub nosed revolver from under the passenger seat and concealed it. Misha had their other handguns in her bag and wrapped the shotgun in a jacket.

They got into the room. Same layout as room 3, he remembered. He jammed a dining chair under the door handle and made sure the window was locked. He heard Misha sniffing from the bathroom. She was sat on the toilet seat, a silent cry, tears rolling down her swollen, bruised up cheek. Wincing as he squatted down to her level. He said nothing, only wrapped his arms around her and held her.

After changing the dressing on his hand, with the help of Misha, he popped some painkillers and lay on the bed. Misha showered, poured herself a bourbon from the mini bar, and sat on the bed. Her head resting against the wall, eyes closed as she sipped her drink.

'Why would Manny give The Arc our location?' She spoke, eyes closed, resting.

'I have no idea. Manny will have to wait.' He replied. His eyes heavy. Exhausted. 'He has done something I never thought would never happen.'

Chapter 21

'Daddy!' Emily shouted, standing, her hands reaching to him. Her face stained red with blood. He smelled the smoke; it burned in his nose. Her scream filled his head.

He sat bolt upright. Soaked in his own sweat. It was dark. The only light creeping in through a gap in the blinds, from a lamp in the lot outside. He could hear the deep breathing of Misha as she slept next to him.

He got himself up. Noted that he wasn't as sore as earlier. The hand throbbed whenever he moved it or used it. He heard Misha's breathing change as he walked around the bed, she was aware of him moving around. His heart, still pounded from seeing Emily. He looked at himself in the mirror and turned on the water. His face, already showing signs of healing. His mind on the nanomachines, wondering how much of it was their doing. As the water filled the bath, he wondered if they would get out of it alive. Misha wasn't supposed to happen. He would eliminate The Arc of Evermore. He had hoped he would die in the process. If not, he planned to eat his own gun. For the first time he acknowledged that there may be a future beyond all this. Misha had happened. He was glad she was in his life.

He lay in the bath, soaking up the warmth from the water. The mirror, steamed up, offered no view but he knew she stood in the doorway. It was a few minutes before she spoke. 'Okay if I come in?'

'Sure, are you alright?' He asked.

'Yeah, pain has eased, headache is gone.' She walked in and sat on the edge of the bath. Her gaze locked on his body. The bruises on his abdomen, moving, augmented by the ripples of the water from where she sat.

'Eyes up.' He joked, smiling at her.

'They look two days old, the bruising, the cuts.' She spoke as she dipped her hand into the water, making a swirl on the surface. 'I know it's bad, what they did to you, the serum, but it seems to help.'

'If we get out of this thing alive, and I want to.' He held her hand as he sat forward. 'We will need to disappear; the law won't make any exemptions.'

'I know, I know. I'll go wherever you go.' Misha said, softly.

'I was prepared to die doing this, I did not expect you to come along. Feel the way I do. I would have shot myself after taking them down.' He scooped up some water and rinsed his hair and beard. 'I need to get us out of this alive.'

Misha made instant coffee for them both as Alex scrolled through his cell phone.

'What was that reporters name, on the news a few nights ago, talking about The Arc?' He asked.

'Gina Santos, I think.' She handed him his coffee. 'They usually have contact details on the network.'

Alex typed her name into his search. He found an email address for the reporter and started composing a message. He employed some buzz words in the message, spoke of shocking the nation, what The Arc of Evermore were doing to innocent women and children, he hoped it would be enough to get a bite from Santos. He left his burner number for her reply.

They drank their coffee, the news playing on the tv, nothing reported about the events at Walker-Mills farm. They ordered pizza from a local place. It arrived lukewarm but they were both too hungry to care or complain.

The cell buzzed at the side of the bed. No caller ID. Alex picked up the call. 'Yeah.' He spoke.

'This is Gina Santos. I believe you have something for me?' A strong Spanish twist on her words.

'I do. I'll assume this call is being recorded?' He knew, but asked anyway, testing her.

'Yes, it is, now what do I call you? You certainly know who I am.' She had begun her information dive process.

'My name is not important. It is what I have that is.' He got up and paced the room as he continued. 'You will meet me, in a public place. Alone. I will provide you with files on The Arc of Evermore and what they have done to innocent people. Do you have a technology specialist? That you can trust?'

Her tone had changed. Intrigue. Excitement, he wondered. 'Yes, I have someone. Where do you propose we meet? I am licensed to carry, try anything and I will shoot you, you need to know that.'

'You will not be harmed. 08:00am tomorrow. The strip mall, 10 miles south of Jackton airfield.' He ended the call.

He removed the cloning device that Manny had given him from Misha's bag. Plugged it into the cell phone Manny had used to send the info and track him. A tiny green LED blinked as it worked. 'She can have these. Her tech person will get everything they need.'

Misha had Santos's profile showing on her cell phone. 'She had been digging on The Arc for a few years now. A lot of dead ends.' She showed him. 'Could make her hit the big time.'

'Or get her killed.' Alex ran his fingers through his hair. 'I don't want that, but I think it could flush out Jupiter.'

They finished the last of the pizza. The clock said 02:18am. They went back to bed, trying to get some sleep before the meeting with Santos.

Chapter 22

The strip mall consisted of eight separate units. Not all of them had vendors, some boarded up, venture gone bust maybe. A coffee shop, fast food counter and a mid-range clothing store the most notable of the occupied units. They made a deliberate effort to get there early. It would allow a window to observe the area, the people, for anything out of the ordinary.

Misha ordered herself a coffee as Alex browsed the neighbouring unit for some more clothes, he had what was on his back, the rest gone with the events at the cabin. 'Hi, two medium Lattes to go please.' She spoke to the barista.

The barista wore hooded, sympathetic eyes as she looked at her face. 'Ma'am, do you need somewhere private? Abuse is not okay; I can call the Police for you?'

'Yeah, the answer to that is no.' Her face warm, blushing. 'We were in a car wreck.' She smiled through the embarrassment. 'I got off lightly, always wear a seatbelt, right?' A natural communicator, she had the knack of disarming people with her wit and directness.

The woman's face matching Misha's in embarrassment. 'I'm so sorry ma'am, I need to mind my own business, I just thought...'

'No, no don't be silly, you were just looking out for another woman. Honest, I'm fine, I carry a gun so no man's gonna beat me.' Misha chuckled, trying to ease the woman's suffering as she looked as thought she needed a fire alarm or the very ground she stood upon to open up and take her.

The woman prepared the two coffees as Alex walked in behind Misha. She noticed the trauma he had also worn on his face. It didn't matter if she believed it or not. They did not need the police interfering at this point.

'Two lattes, please, on the house.' She waved away the cash Misha offered. 'I must be more careful with customers, please enjoy.'

Misha stuffed twenty bucks into the tip jar. 'Thank you, Melody.' She said, reading her name badge on her apron.

They sat in the car sipping their coffee when Santos pulled in. Late model Prius. Gun metal grey. She was alone, scanning the area are she parked her car. A quick call to someone on her cell before she exited the car. A Safety thing, Alex assumed.

He was already out the car as Misha watched him get to within a few metres of Santos as she walked toward the units.

'Gina. Don't turn. The bench, ahead. Take a seat.' He spoke as he walked by her side.

She did as he asked. She was a good looking, tan woman. Latin blood. He saw a fire in her eyes as he sat next to her on the bench.

'Take this cell phone and cloning device. It has information on individuals, different roles in The Arc, most of them dead. The locations are used by them, for various reasons. The cell has photos from inside the industrial unit the cops bust the other day. They use women to give them babies and harvest their blood.' Alex spoke facing ahead. He knew she craned her neck to get a better view of his face.

'How did you come by this? What good are the identities of dead cultists to me?' Santos asked. 'I've known some of what they do to people, could never prove it, they have government officials in bed with them.'

'I was there. I've cloned every single cell phone or computer that was accessible after I ended them.' Alex turned to face her. 'Don't let yourself get killed over this.'

'Did they do that to your face? What do you want for this information? What do you need in return?' Her dark eyes boring a hole into him. Assessing him.

'Yes. I want you to use it to expose them.' He stood and moved where she did not have to turn to see him.

'And what do you get out of it?' She demanded.

'I get to kill every last one of them. They took something from me, that can never be replaced. Do not report anything on Duke's bar until I call you.' He broke eye contact and started to walk away from her.

'Shit. You are him.' She got up and walked after him. 'You are the Nothingman!'

Alex continued walking. Misha swung the Jeep around. He opened the door and jumped into the passenger seat. They drove off as Gina Santos stood, a subtle smile etched on her face.

'Let's get a window for this thing.' Alex said as he searched for a junkyard nearby. The wind was blowing Misha's hair around as if she was on a theme park ride.

A hundred and twenty dollars lighter. They left the junkyard with a replacement window for the driver's side. Alex changed into some fresh, clean clothes as Misha drove. Black jeans and an oversized t shirt, also black, he had picked up at the store.

'Let's go see Manny.' He stared out the window at passing cars. 'He won't be there, but he will know when we are.'

'Will you kill him?' Misha asked direct and to the point.

'I have no idea. I don't want to, but I need to know what the hell he was thinking.' He considered the act of killing his best friend. In an angry state, he thought he could do it. He rationalised, surely there was a reason, had they found him out, threatened to kill him if he didn't give them something? He thought many options over, as they headed towards his house.

It looked no different from the last time either of them had visited. Alex would be shocked if he was still around. He scribbled something down on the back of his clothes receipt with a sharpie and got out of the car. A quick reassuring feel at the pistol sat at the small of his back. A glance up and down the street for anything different. Parked cars. A delivery truck, parked up with two overweight men eating something in the cab. No threat.

He didn't knock or wait at the door for anyone. He kicked the door near the lock, and it sprang open. Gun drawn in a flash, he kept low and swept the room. No Manny. His computer setup powered off. The small LED of a cctv camera sat atop the centre screen. Alex said nothing, leaned into the camera holding a piece of paper. It read, we need to talk and had his burner number written at the bottom.

Alex ripped the hard drive out of the base unit and walked out of the house. The door left half open behind him. Misha hadn't entered the house and got back into the car as soon as she saw Alex come out.

He tossed the hard drive onto the back seat as Misha pulled the car away from the kerb.

'He was watching.' Alex unravelled the bandage from his hand. Assessing the wound from the nail gun. 'A camera. He will be worried that I took his hard drive, made sure he saw me take it.'

'What will you do with it?' Misha asked.

'I'll destroy it. My old identity is there. The details of what Truman and Waller did to me. I can't allow that to get out. I just hope Manny doesn't realise how valuable that information will be.' Alex shook his head. He wished this was avoidable.

They been on the road for 21 minutes when the cell phone rang. No caller ID. He wondered if it was Santos or Manny.

'You have my attention.' It was Manny.

'You are going to meet me and explain why you fed us to the wolves. Are you one of them?' Alex maintained his calm. He knew Manny could read him. He wasn't usually far off the mark when it came to Alex.

'Shut your fucking mouth with that kinda shit.' Manny shouted down the phone. 'I ain't no Arc man.'

'Then why, Manny?' Alex demanded.

'There are some things you need to hear. You need to be educated. You need to be reminded.' Manny sounded off, with a venomous tone to his voice.

'Where, When?' Alex had placed him on speaker as he asked.

'Alright. The multistorey on 33rd street. 3pm. Tomorrow. You see it's high enough you won't have the fox pick me off from distance. She around?' Manny let out a laugh. Always the smartest man in the room, he thought, wrongly. 'Bring her along man, she needs to hear this shit also. If either of you are packing, I'll let our mutual friends know where you are. Again.' The call was ended.

'What a dick, I never thought for a moment he would do this. I mean, I've known him days, a week at most but, no way.' Misha spoke, conflicted with thinking out loud.

'Over twenty-five years I've known him. I never saw it coming either, Misha.' Alex worked the radio until he found something he liked. 'Clarence is gonna be happy to see us again.' He laughed.

They headed back for another night at the Motel when his phone buzzed again. No Called ID. He answered, staying silent.

'This is gold, Nothingman.' It was Gina Santos. 'Who is your guy? This is high level hacking. Data mining. I want to meet him. There must be more'

An idea entered his head straight away. Manny wanted him and Misha there, but he didn't stipulate who else. '3pm. Tomorrow. Multistorey on 33rd street.' He ended the call.

'Alex, what the ...?' Misha, wide eyed stopped before using profanity.

'I'll give him his chance to make this right.' He adjusted the volume to hear the song playing on the radio. It was Yellow Ledbetter by Pearl Jam. The guitar introduction, a thing of musical genius.

Chapter 22

His anxiety levels crept up as they made their way along 33rd street. It wasn't the prospect of seeing Manny. It was where Sarah and Emily had been caught in a car bombing. The shops still wore the mark of the event. Boarded up. Closed until further notice. He was sure Misha knew why he slowed the vehicle as they passed by. Dead flowers laid against the shopfronts. Withered to a tenth of their size. The wax of candles left by mourners or passers-by still stuck to the sidewalk. He felt a thud in his chest as his heart raced. Chest tightening. His breathing was faster. His fingers tingling as he gripped the steering wheel. The soft touch of Misha's hand on the back of his neck brought him back down. He slowed his breathing. He flexed and extended his fingers, working out the tingling.

He knew Manny would make an extra effort to be there first. To ensure his safety. Alex didn't blame him for that. He wondered if Santos too, would have tried to be there early. When they spoke the day before, he could tell she was irked by him getting the drop on her. She was used to being in control.

It was a 5-level parking lot in the shopping precinct of the town. A barrier-controlled entrance and exit sat on the street level, allowing access to the spiral concourse that led to each level. Manny was right it was the tallest structure in the immediate area, less chance of being shot by a sniper.

He parked the Jeep across the road from the lot. Paid at the meter and stuck his receipt to the windscreen. They had already stuffed their guns under the front seats of the car. Alex had already stripped the hard drive and smashed the circuits within and thrown them into a bin at the Motel. The hard drive, in his hand as he walked, looked like a complete article but was quite the contrary.

They took the stairs to the top level. The smell of human piss in the stairwell was overpowering. As he swung the door open at the top, he saw the sky. Grey. Brooding. Angry. Waiting to drop millions of raindrops upon them. Manny, in his wheelchair was at the opposite end, facing the door they used. He saw Santos' Prius parked up near where Manny was waiting.

Manny was within 20 feet when Santos got out of her car. Manny wheeled his head around to see who it was.

'What the fuck is this, Alex?' He shouted.

Santos looked at Manny and then to Alex. A puzzled look upon her face.

'Gina Santos, this is Manny Johnson. My data guy.' He smiled as he said it.

'Misha brings me a friend, finally?' Manny laughed through gritted teeth. His anger simmering.

Gina Santos spoke to Manny. 'Pendejo, Fuck you!' She turned to Alex. 'Please tell me what is going on here!'

'Well. Gina Santos. This guy falls into a lake of shit and comes up shiny new. He falls into a pit of vipers and comes out without a mark!' Manny spat as he spoke. 'He fucking gets iced in the sandbox and comes out a fucking picture of health! He drives us near an IED and guess what? I end up in a fuckin chair. Pissing into a bag. Can't get my dick hard ever again!' He waved hands in an animated fashion. 'The fucking wife dies; he gets an upgrade within a couple weeks!' Pointing at Misha.

'This what it's all about Manny? Are you serious?' Alex could feel the veins bulging in his neck as he reeled from the hatred in Manny's words. 'You gave them our location. More than once! We could have been killed you piece of shit.'

'This is not what I came here for.' Santos held her hands up.

'Shut the fuck up bitch!' Manny yelled.

Gina Santos stood defiant. She looked at Manny with hatred in her eyes. She was not used to being spoken to like that.

'Money talks when you have nothing else Alex. We split the accounts of those Arc douchebags. It wasn't enough. They caught me snooping. Offered a million to give you up.' Manny spoke like he believed he was right, entitled to it. 'Now give me my fucking hard drive or I'll drop this text and they'll come here for you.'

Alex considered picking him up and throwing him over the edge. He pictured it in his head. 'Here.' He tossed the hard drive into Manny's lap. 'Make this right Manny. Work with Gina give her everything you have on the Arc.'

'Fuck you.' Manny barked.

Alex turned and walked a few paces away. His head in his hands. He heard a gasp and turned back to face him. Misha held her hands out in front in an attempt to de-escalate the situation. Manny held a handgun. It was pointed at Alex. Before he could say a word, he fired. Alex dropped to a squat position. Hands by his head. Two more shots rang out. He heard Misha's scream.

He looked at her. She still stood. Unmoving, she had her eyes on him. He ran his hands over his body. He wasn't hit.

His eyes darted to Santos. She stood. Gun in hand. Pointed at Manny.

Manny was sat farther back in his seat than usual. Almost sliding out. Blood seeping from two holes in his belly. Dark red spreading across his white sweater.

He looked back to Misha. She mouthed the words; are you okay. He nodded back to her. She rushed toward Gina, wrapping her arm around her, gently taking her by the wrist. Easing the gun down from her ready stance.

Alex walked over to Manny. He was alive. His breathing was laboured. The gun laying by his wheel. After lifting his sweater, he knew he would be dead soon.

'Alex. Man. Take me to a fucking hospital.' Manny tried to grab him as he spoke.

Alex said nothing.

'C'mon man.' Manny begun to cry. 'You owe me man. You fucking owe me!'

Alex walked away from him. He could hear him strain to grab the gun and decided he was no longer a threat.

'Hey Gina, Are you okay?' He noticed she was crying. 'The gun, is it registered to you?'

'Yes. Yes, all legal.' She answered. Shaking.

'They are going to trace it to you.' Alex said. Looking her in the eye.

She took a deep breath and pulled her cell phone out. Alex watched her dial 911. 'Police and Ambulance please. This is Gina Santos. I have just shot a man who tried to rob me. The multistorey on 33rd. Yes, he is still breathing.' She ended the call. 'You both need to go; it was an exchange gone wrong. He tried to shoot me first.'

'Gina...' Alex began.

'I'll call you when I'm done.' Gina ushered them both to leave the lot.

Alex looked on as Manny was a few inches from reaching his gun. The bleeding inside the abdomen would be catastrophic and a lot more than what they could see. He would be dead before they were in the car.

He held Misha's hand as they crossed the street trying to avoid the eyes of any onlooker. Another gunshot echoed from the parking structure. They got into the Jeep as the sound of sirens could be heard in the distance. He started up the Wrangler and drove as if nothing had happened. Alex punched in Duke's bar to his GPS and followed the route provided.

'I thought he'd killed you.' She sat in the passenger seat. 'How the hell did he miss?' Her head rested in her hands.

'I have no idea. I was going to throw him over the side, he's lucky Santos shot him.' He wondered how he had gotten away without a scratch following today's turn of events.

'You think we can trust her?' Misha looked at him. Worry setting in over her face.

'She shot him. It's her call how much she tells the cops. We might have been caught on the street level camera near the lot.' He looked at her as he was driving. 'No cameras inside the stairwell. We ran away as soon as we heard the first shot.' He placed his hand on hers. He wondered how much more of this she could take. He thought about how much of a person is lost after every single traumatic experience.

It was getting dark as they pulled up outside Duke's bar. It was a simple, dingy looking roadside bar and diner. Small windows. Not much view inside from the parking lot. Dimly lit. He assumed there would be a rear service door, maybe a fire escape door also. He considered the building for a few minutes before pulling out of the lot.

Misha searched the web for a nearby hotel. She punched in the address to the GPS for the Dogwood Plains Resort. It said they were around 35 minutes from it.

Alex thought about the strain being placed upon Misha. The emotional lag that would soon catch up with her. She had never knowingly killed a person before meeting Alex. Now, she had, and watched even more be killed as their relationship progressed. He decided that they would lay low. Under the radar. Take some time to heal up. Then he would call Truman.

Chapter 23

Dogwood Plains was stunning, a resort with a mountainous backdrop, beautiful forests and grassy plains would be enough in a tent, never mind a luxury resort room or lodge. They checked in to the resort under his alias. Another car accident explanation provided to the checking clerk. They paid for lodge accommodation instead of a conventional room. It was a short walk from the main building to a row of purpose built all you need in one place lodges. Theirs was number 20. Set over two levels. Lots of glass allowing the sought-after vista on the horizon. A hot tub on the deck. A jacuzzi bath and rainfall shower. Fully integrated entertainment system. A studio style kitchen and living area took up much of the ground floor. They paid up for a week.

They ordered a BBQ meat platter to the lodge and opened a bottle of Jack Daniels Bourbon. Misha surfed the channels on the massive Tv. She stopped when the face of Gina Santos flashed up behind a newsreader.

'Award winning reporter Gina Santos was involved in a shooting this afternoon where one person has been reported dead. The details are unknown at this time and Gina is said to be fully co-operating with the Police in their enquiries.' The man announced machinelike, rhythmical and rigid in his seat.

Alex and Misha exchanged a glance. Some relief. Some sadness. Manny had betrayed him. This much, was true. He thought of their youth. Their time in the marines. Manny's accident. How he was with Sarah and Emily. He was Uncle Manny to Emily. He could not understand how it had gotten

to a point where Manny saw him as a cash cow. Would he
have been happy to see him murdered by some cult maniac
for money. People change, cliched, they say it all the time, he
thought. He wondered what the third shot was. Was it Manny,
shooting himself? Was it Santos, shooting Manny?

His thoughts were broken by Misha throwing her
underwear onto his lap. She ran upstairs as he looked at her. He
heard water running and followed her upstairs. They sat in the
jacuzzi bath drinking bourbon. They took in the view from the
large windows and drank some more bourbon before Misha
led him to the bed.

He only woke once after seeing Emily again. Her smiling
face, covered in blood. This time she screamed for him as she
was slowly engulfed in flames. The dreams were getting worse,
they felt more real each time. A headache, probably from the
bourbon, droned as soon as he got out of bed. The early
morning sun, hanging low cast across the land as far as the eye
could see. Hazy orange glow raked across the plains, to the
forest and hills in the distance. He pulled on a pair of boxer
shorts, wary that anyone passing could see him standing at the
window. He brought her a glass of water and some painkillers,
assuming she would feel the post alcohol fallout. He studied
her face as she slept. The bruising, over the worst, the cut on
her lip, it would leave a small scar he thought. She was one of
these women who looked good, without makeup. He stroked
her hair and she smiled; eyes still closed.

'Water and some pills on the bedside.' He whispered before
walking out on the deck. The air smelled fresh. A hint of citrus
in the air as a groundskeeper used a motorised saw to trim back
some evergreens that lined the path. An older couple strolled

along the path a few lodges along. He wondered if that was ever going to be possible for him. Misha entered his thoughts. She deserved a future. He thought about Sarah. A curtain of guilt sat heavy on him as thought about Sarah, how she would never be able to take that walk. He could never escape the fact that he wasn't there when they needed him. He questioned if they would have been near 33rd street had he been home. He knew there were some stores there but nothing either Sarah or Emily would regularly visit. He sat on the step that led down to the path and watched some birds peck and feed at some seed someone had thrown. The high-pitched call of a hawk made the birds flee into the trees.

Hodges. Muller. Andersen. Sarah. Emily. Earl. Manny. He thought of each of their deaths. The common denominator was him. He had dealt in death when he was deployed overseas and now, on home soil he was still immersed in death. The cultists that he had murdered were what stood between him and progress. Progress, no matter how small was a mission he was accustomed to since he was a boy. His father had always told him to keep on moving forward. No matter how far. An inch. A footstep, it all mattered. Thinking of his father, the man was far from perfect. His father struck him several times, it was less than some of his childhood friends' fathers, so he thought that itself was a small victory. He drank too much on occasion which only fuelled his high expectations and demands of Alex's mother. He worked too much, away more than he was home. Alex knew that he used his father as the rough pencil line guide, a baseline of which he would surpass in his own duty as a father to Emily. He was too involved, selfish, damaged even, to have noticed he had he hadn't fallen too far from the tree.

His failure wasn't in violence towards Emily or her mother, it was that he too, spent most of his time away working or as an absent shell reliving what had happened when he was away. He tried to accept that he had his chance. He wished there was a do-over button. It was gone. Living the rest of his life knowing his choices, behaviours and inability to stop and live in the moment, to stop and smell the air, listen to the bird calls, be a friend, a husband, a father had shaped and sculpted the moment he found himself in. He would hurt every single minute of every day until his heart stopped. This was about the only thing he knew was certain.

Alex got up and walked back inside the lodge. The smell of bacon, was strong. Misha stood over the burner teasing a pan of bacon. Eggs sat cooking in a separate pan. 'There's a message for you.' She waved a spatula. 'The Truman one I think.'

There was a notification of the screen. It was the only contact on the cell. Ed Truman. He had simply written call me.

Alex hit the call button. Ed Truman picked up on the second ring. 'Brody. Do you still look like you have been excavated from a grave?' He sniffed. 'You know, the face, is it presentable?'

'Well. It's better than yesterday. The eye is unhindered by the swelling.' Alex stared at himself as he spoke in the reflection of a window. He thought about a grave, whether his be a hole in the ground dug by a hired killer or something worse.

'I need you to meet someone. Alone. No Misha.' Truman could be heard tapping in the background. 'It's not a personal fuckin thing. The guy doesn't need to know about her. It'll protect her.'

Alex sighed. Looking at Misha as she cooked. 'When? Who is it?'

'Not on the fuckin phone. 17:00pm. The hangar. Do not be late.' Truman ended the call.

Misha turned to the sound of the cell phone bouncing onto the couch. 'You wanna eat in here or on the deck?' She turned with eggs and bacon plated up in each hand.

He took a plate. A nod. 'The deck, I'll come back in for the coffee, you go on out.'

They ate their breakfast as the sun reached a high vantage point, an overwatch position, where it would observe their world for the rest of today. Most of the haziness had burned off. She asked. 'Ed, what does he need now?'

'To meet someone. He requested that you don't come with me.' He assessed her face for a reaction. 'Said you will be safer if this third party knows nothing about you or your involvement.'

'You trust him?' Looking into his eyes.

'Yes and no. He proved something at the farm. If his issue was with you, he could have delayed his riding in on a white horse act.' Sipping his coffee before speaking again. 'If going alone keeps you safe from someone else, then that is what needs to be done.'

The rest of the day was spent between walking together on the resort paths and trails and laying up on the couch. He left an hour before the meet. To control any variables.

Chapter 24

The airfield was no different to any other time he had been there. Several vehicles were already parked up. It was 16:45pm. The door was opened for him as he approached by one of Truman's guys. The main hangar door was closed over. He noticed the Lear jet first. Then the kerosine like smell of jet fuel diluted the air. Truman was mid-way between his office and the door waving Alex over. He said nothing until they were in his office. Door closed. 'Our mutual friend got here early.' Truman stood cleaning his glasses with his shirt. 'He's a fan of your work.' Truman walked to the window that looked onto the hangar floor. 'He is on a call. In the jet.' Truman was nervous, that made Alex uneasy. He offered nothing in return. 'Brody. Who the fuck is Manny Johnson?'

That caught him off guard. Lying to Truman would be the first roll of dice in a very dangerous game. 'A friend. I had him working on finding Harvey Jupiter. Exposing The Arc.'

'Hmm.' Truman lit a cigar. 'Then why did he fucking contact me?' He took a long draw on the cigar. The end sizzling quietly as the orange glow worked its way closer to his mouth. 'He wanted a meet. Things to discuss he said.' He flicked ash on the floor. 'I had a guy investigate him. My fuckin name came back on some fuckin deep dives.' He stopped speaking as the stairs of the jet deployed. The thud echoed throughout the structure.

Alex still stood; he looked through the window. A dark-skinned man, around 6 foot 3, and 220lbs walked toward the office. He could see Vice President Marcus Hall still looked after himself. A perfectly tailored suit wrapped his frame to perfection. The former U.S Marine was picked up by the Denver Broncos and managed 2 seasons as Line-backer before blowing his knee out, ending his football career. Still sporting the military buzz cut, he wore a thin, well-maintained goatee with a few speckled grey hairs throughout.

'Ed. Are you well?' Marcus linked to Truman in a casual, familiar handshake. 'I apologise for the untimely nature of my call.'

'No need to apologise sir.' Truman held his hands up. He turned to Alex. 'This is Alex Brody. The Nothingman.'

Alex stood, looking at the Vice President. 'I am a fan of your recent work Mr Brody.' Marcus held his hand out. 'Pleased to meet you.'

Alex shook his hand. 'Nice to meet you sir.'

'You understand the nature of the work Ed provides?' Marcus spoke as he was handed a cigar from Truman. 'It is essential to the national security of our great nation. Accolades cannot be given. Credit is impossible. If you die or worse, get caught, you will not be helped.'

'I understand sir.' Alex wondered how much to say.

'Sit down, son. Let's cut the shit.' Marcus sat in Trumans chair. 'Ed here has recruited you for specific reasons. I do not need to know unless you want to discuss these things. Nothingman, my understanding is that you have lost all that you have, this makes you a unique asset. Unafraid to die.' His face trying to read Alex as every word is spoken. 'You intrigue me. What you have done to that monstrous organisation in such short time. It's refreshing to know we have you.'

'My family were murdered by The Arc. Whilst I lay in a bed getting pumped full of Composite Nano Serum B after getting blown up in the sandbox.' Alex felt a sudden shift, the atmosphere in the room changed. Truman's posture changed, as did Hall's.

Vice President Marcus Hall was on his feet in a second. Trumans table flipped as he demonstrated tremendous power. Ed Truman had sprung to his feet to avoid being hit by the table. 'What the fuck Ed? What the fuck did I tell you! Stop the fucking trials. Stop the fucking trials!'

'Marcus, calm down, it worked. He is living proof.' Truman held a hand towards Alex.

The Vice President showcased his speed as he moved to the window and dropped the blinds. 'You two are going to have plenty to discuss after I leave.' He adjusted his jacket that had unbuttoned as he expressed his anger. 'Alex, you mind if I call you Alex?' He continued regardless. 'I will not explain what he did to you. It was not under my instruction or any agenda of the United States of America. What I need to know, what I need you to know.' He got closer to Alex as he sat. 'Harvey Jupiter, if you can find him, will lead you to someone currently in office. We believe a Senator. They need to be exposed and dealt with. The latter part, I leave to your discretion.' Marcus Hall rubbed his forehead. 'Thank you.' He said before walking out the office. A wave of his hand signalled a few men to open the hangar doors.

Ed stood looking at Alex. His posture, anxious. 'How long have you known?' He looked as if he steadied himself for an assault.

'It doesn't matter.' Alex decided not to move. 'You should just cut the shit Ed. We are too far along now to split hairs.'

'The op in the middle east. Lead car, you, got hit. I could not believe you survived. I took a fucking gamble and got you out.' Truman spoke as he worked his way around the upturned table to sit across from Alex. 'You were gonna be fucking half vegetable, I forced Waller to give you the Serum.' He turned to watch the Lear jet be towed out of the hangar. 'Everyone else died we gave it to. You fuckin healed up quick. Neurological process fuckin better than ever.' He trembled as he lit another cigar. 'I need you to look from my fucking view here, before I keep talking.' He looked at Alex for affirmation. 'An asset is more use when they have nothing to live for. Your wife and kid, sealed your deal, I'm sorry, that's how we get a perfect asset.' He looked as though he still expected to be assaulted. 'It's the way it is, I'm sorry they died, but it led us to this fuckin moment. On the way to removing the head of a fuckin abomination.' Truman shuffled in his chair. 'These cult fucks get further embedded on capitol hill; Hall doesn't get the big chair. See where I'm going?'

'It's unethical. An abuse of power. However, I understand this is how you operate. Outside the law, outside process, the CIA have a track record of this kind of shit.' Alex waved away cigar smoke that hovered in front of his face. 'Let's say I get this done. No more Arc. What happens to me?' His eyes boring a hole into Truman, a hint of a lie, a hesitation would be all it took for Alex to launch himself at Truman and crush his throat with his bare hands.

Truman did not move. He did not blink. He relaxed his posture as he spoke. 'You go away. Somewhere you won't be recognised. You can take my help to get you gone or you can disappear yourself. 'He pushed his glasses back up to the bridge of his nose. 'One thing is a certainty though, if I need you, I will come calling. If the VP needs you, I will come calling.' The words were said coldly, calmly with purpose. Alex considered this the most honest Truman had been since they met. 'If you decide to eat your gun. That's on you.'

'Can you get me another vehicle?' Alex stood and stretched out his neck.

'What do you want?' Truman smirked.

'Something inconspicuous. 4 doors ideally.' He walked to where Trumans desk lay and returned it to its desired position.

'Give me a few hours. Where do you want it delivered?' Truman got up and pulled his cell phone from his pocket.

'Duke's bar parking lot. Leave something on the dash so I know what one it is. Put the key in the tailpipe.' A nod to Truman as he walked out.

Truman followed him to the door before speaking. 'There is a bag on your seat. Call it a fuckin advance or whatever.'

A bag sat on his seat, as Truman had said. He unzipped it and looked inside. Several new identities, passports and drivers' licences bound with elastic bands sat on top of at least ten rolls of cash. He felt under his seat for his gun. It was unmoved, sat in the same pocket of fabric.

His thoughts filled his head. The Vice President of the United States of America, advocating for severe violence and an any means necessary approach to eliminate a sick cult. A caveat some might say, was the leader of The Arc being his direct competition for the next oval office seat. Alex thought the odds of pure, honest coincidence were less than winning the lottery without ever buying a ticket. Most people discussed this kind of clandestine activity tongue in cheek. Not really knowing that it is going on but done so more in an exercise of mistrust in the powers that be. An alternative view from the more patriotic stance could favour the ideations of Marcus Hall, going to the extreme to deal with an extreme. A threat to the stability, safety and security of the people has traditionally sparked wars, riots and some other activities that were censored and taken to the graves of the people involved.

He was concerned that they need a Nothingman. That they would do anything to maintain that status. Truman requested that Misha not be involved in the meeting, it would be safer he went as far as saying. The expendable assets usually fit the mould of unmarried, unattached, no children, less likely to have issues making horrible decisions, ethics and a moral compass that didn't function. Nobody to miss them when they are gone.

Back at the resort, he saw Misha through the huge glass window. She looked untroubled, she moved around the kitchen area, dancing as she wiped down the surfaces. He made the assumption she was playing music; she sang along to something. His pace slowed, he was enjoying it, she was fluid, carefree and looked genuinely happy. Her eyes caught him before he footed the first step up to the deck, she put a little more into her dancing and singing. It was an 80's song by Jermaine Stewart. Something about not taking your clothes off to have a good time. He had an internal argument whether to tell her about the meeting or not.

'Hey you.' Smiling, holding a beer out to him.

'Hey, you mind giving me a bourbon if you are gonna keep singing.' He blocked her soft jab and took the beer.

'Everything okay? Using her hands to lift herself up on the marbled countertop. She sipped her own bottle of beer.

'How much do you want to know?' standing close to her. Her perch on the counter nullifying his height advantage. They were now even.

She took a long pull on the beer. Shrugged her shoulders. 'I don't need protected, but I trust you. Tell me what you think I should know.'

'Marcus Hall.' Is all he said. He drained his beer and grabbed another from the refrigerator. 'His challenger for the oval office is Harvey Jupiter's boss.' The metallic clink of his bottle cap hitting the marble filled his pause. 'A senator, identity unknown.'

'Wow. I thought there would be some bigwig involved, maybe local, but a Senator?' She held his hand, inspecting the damage from the nail gun. 'You think after all that, they'll allow us out alive?'

'Truman told me, I disappear after it, he's given new ID's and cash.' A nod to the bag sat at the door. 'Says services can be retained though, himself or Hall, they call, they'll expect me to work.'

'Is there a version of all this where we get to be together?' Her body language tense, stressed. 'We both know the best kind of assets are expendable.'

He didn't know how to answer that. Before he could apply logic, she lowered herself down to standing on the floor. 'I'm sorry, I shouldn't have asked that... I ...' Quickly breaking off and heading upstairs.

He knew she was able to risk assess. She had already made a choice to be with him. To embark on his campaign against The Arc of Evermore. He had already considered trying to drive her away, for her safety, to ensure she had some sort of future. Yes, they could disappear after all this, but it would never be a normal life.

The failing he made with Sarah. Keeping his emotions boiled up. Hiding the trauma. He thought he protected her, but it served as a wedge, adding stress to their relationship, he spoke less, was withdrawn. It carried over to his ability to be a father, he could not allow these failings to set a course destined to have the same outcome. He decided that pushing Misha away would be the selfish thing to do.

He briefed Misha and they went out a drive. He set eyes on a 4-door sedan that sat in the parking lot at Duke's. A cigar box laid on the dash, Truman's brand. Key, sitting where he had asked it to be left. He parked the jeep next to it and handed Misha the keys.

'I need you as my eyes, anyone shady arrives, buzz my phone. Any law enforcement, draw them away, make a 911 call nearby, whatever it takes. It could get messy, and it's public. Between Truman, The Deacon and Manny, all info suggests that this is a meet point for members and an intel drop off point.'

They spent no longer taking it all in than was necessary. They returned to the resort and tried to relax and make the most of the time.

Chapter 25

He sat at the booth, with his unfinished whisky. The call the cop had been despatched to was likely Misha, drawing him away as they'd agreed.

'Is it itchy?' The little girl, peeking over the booth asked.

'Sir, I am so sorry. Amy, leave the man alone!' The mother, embarrassed at her daughter's direct approach. An approach that children seem to be able to get away with more than adults do.

'It's fine, honest, is what itchy?' He asked the girl.

'Your beard. My daddies was itchy.' She giggled.

'Oh no, not anymore, I use a good shampoo.' Smiling, she reminded him a little of Emily.

The bartender approached the woman and little girl. The first thing Alex noticed was the tattoo. The Arc and Greek letter E. There was now no doubt in his mind he was in the right place.

'What'll it be ladies?' The man slurred. His eyes poured over them both as they sat.

'Two sodas, two club sandwiches please.' She replied.

Alex watched as the bar man made a note, he turned to walk away and flipped a hand signal to the three men playing pool. They returned a nod. They thought they were smart or felt safe enough to practice their darkness, Alex wondered which it was. He felt nauseated, he knew something bad was on the cards.

'Excuse me, would you mind it at all if I used the restroom, Amy is refusing to come with.' The lady stood at the edge of the booth, totally unaware of what could happen in this place. Her face a little flushed.

'Sure, I'll make sure she doesn't leave or order any alcohol.' He laughed. A bad feeling rising inside him.

She told the child she was going to use the restroom, asking her again to go alongside her. The girl shook her head while she stirred her water using a straw. A blend of embarrassment and thanks danced across the woman's face as she sheepishly made her way toward the restroom.

The woman had barely passed the three men at the pool table, and they had flashed a hand signal to the bar tender. He nodded back to them as the door closed behind her. Was it permission, was it acknowledgement? Alex wondered.

'Hey, how old are you? An inquisitive look on his face as he spoke.

'Seven. One birthday before eight.' The girl answered, blowing air through her straw into the glass.

'Do you think you could help me with something? Pulling his keys from his pocket. A quick glance towards the restrooms. Two of the three men were heading towards the door.

'Yeah, I think I can.' The girl said. 'I help my mom all the time.'

'So, your mommy, bought my car from me, I need to you to go check the lights flash when you press this button, but you need to be really close to it okay?' He demonstrated what button to press. His heart racing as he heard the door to the restrooms close behind the men. He knew there was a risk sending the girl outside but he had no choice, she did not deserved to see of hear what was about to happen.

'Okay.' She ambled off her chair and headed out to the parking lot. He could hear her clicking the button all the way through to the Door. The barman was trying not to follow her with his eyes. He sensed that there may be a problem.

Alex got up, drank his whisky like a shot. He drew a deep breath and walked towards the restroom. He was a few feet from the third man playing pool when he looked up and saw him. 'Hey, man. Restrooms outta use. Try somewhere else.' His yellow rat like teeth visible before the smell of rotting teeth hit Alex in the face.

'No. I think I'll be using the restroom pal.' He stood within striking distance of the man. Two loud thuds on the bar. The barman signalling to the other patrons that it was time to leave. They scurried out the door, something told Alex this was not the first time.

Alex had already decided what he was going to do to the rat like man, but the bar man was significantly farther away. The last of the patrons had left the establishment, announced by the slamming of the door.

Alex knew the man was going to try punch him before the man did. He quickly pulled his knife from his pocket and drove it down through the man's hand and into the pool table. Before the man could react or scream, he launched an open palm into the man's throat and he crumbled to the ground, hand stuck to the table as he sagged, lifelessly. The sound of metal dragging on wood prompted him to grab a ball from the table. In one fluid movement he launched the ball at the bar tender. The wet, dull noise as it struck his right eye reverberated from one end of the bar to the other. He hit the ground with a thud. The aluminium baseball bat followed him.

Alex pushed through the restroom door, and he heard the woman pleading with the two men inside the female restroom. He kicked the door open; it surprised the three of them in the room. Knife, right hand, it would take three steps and a well-placed blow to stop the first of the two men. The other, stood with his penis in one hand, his other hand had a loop of the woman's hair wrapped around it as he tried to force her to her knees.

'Not your fuckin business, man, fuck off!' The knife wielding man screamed. He took his eyes off Alex for a mere second. That was all he needed.

He was on the man faster than anyone in the room could have foreseen. A quick manipulation of the man's wrist allowed him to make the man stab himself in the neck, directed by Alex. As he dropped to the floor his buddy started to turn towards Alex. He stepped in close and drove the knife into the man's hand that was on his penis. He squealed like a wounded animal as his hand was pinned to his groin area via his penis. Alex headbutted the man in the face sending him backwards, crashing through the ceramic washbasin to the floor.

'Hey, you are okay, I need to you breathe.' Holding the woman's chin up. He needed the eye contact. She had to understand what he was about to say. 'Amy is fine, she is standing by a black Jeep Wrangler in the lot.' Brushing her hair off her face. Closing the buttons on her top as he spoke. 'She has the keys, take the car, get somewhere safe. There is a few thousand dollars in the centre console.'

Tears streaming down her cheeks. 'Oh my god, thank you thank you!'

'Take the back exit when you leave here.' Holding the door open.

'What about you? Your car?' Sniffling between words.

'It's okay, just go, take it, keep it, whatever you need to do to get you and your daughter safe, do it!' He nodded, ending the conversation as she hurried out the restroom.

He looked at the men laying on the floor. The first one was dead, in a pool of blood from his neck, Arc tattoo on the wrist. The other breathed heavily, laying on broken ceramic. He dragged him off the debris, another Arc tattoo. He made some noises as he began to regain consciousness. Alex splashed water on his face as he lay bleeding from where the knife had penetrated.

'The drops. I know they are done here. Where will I find them?' He grabbed the man's bloodied face.

'Fuck you.' The man spat.

Alex stamped his foot on the knife handle, driving it farther into the man's hand, penis, and groin. He squealed again in agony. 'Do I need to ask again you sick piece of shit?'

'Gents. Second stall. Behind the panel. Now please...' Before the man could finish Alex drove the heel of his boot into the man's throat, ending his life.

As he had said. A large, folded envelope sat behind the panel. He grabbed it and headed back into the bar area. The rat like man still dangled from his stuck hand in the pool table. Alex pulled his knife, dropping the man to the floor. He looked up the bar and saw the bar man sitting with his back rested against the bar, thumbing a cell phone. He walked to the window to check that his Jeep was gone before walking up the bar to where the bar tender sat. The right side of his face was caved in. His eye ruptured and undistinguishable amongst the tissue and blood weeping from his wound. He breathed loudly from his mouth and spat the occasional blood clot as Alex walked towards him.

'Warning someone important?' An optimistic tone in his voice.

'You are dead, you can't stop us.' Slurring. Spitting. Looking up with his only eye.

He could hear the low hum of a motor entering the parking lot. 'I'm supposed to be dead, so you are sort of right.' He snatched the cell phone and read the message that was already sent. It was only two words. Red One. 'Who's coming?'

'It won't matter.' He laughed quietly. The sound of footsteps nearing the door.

The door opened letting in some welcome daylight. Misha's body silhouetted with the contrast od the dark bar and daylight behind. 'That cop might be back soon, he won't find the crash, your car was gone, I wasn't sure if you had gone already.'

'Yeah, this animal and his friends were about to do something unspeakable. I gave the car to the woman and child to get away.' He pointed to where the man sat behind the bar.

Misha peered over the bar and screwed up her face as she laid eyes on the grotesque injuries the man wore on his face. The low wail of a siren could be heard in the distance.

'Might need a gun.' He nodded to Misha.

Misha walked back out the bar to grab a gun from the car. Alex picked up the baseball bat that lay next to the man. He had a sick grin on his face. Until Alex drove the bat down into the top of his skull.

The door opened and he caught the Glock as Misha tossed it to him. She walked back out to the car as the sirens stopped. He was close. Alex walked around and took a seat. He opened the envelope and began to look through its contents. Several sensitive documents, official Police transcripts. Providing warning to any Arc sites under Police scrutiny, dates of busts and names of officers involved. Addresses of vulnerable women for recruitment, he shuddered at the thought of how deep this depravity ran. He now knew why the cop had visited earlier.

The cruiser entered the lot following its altered silent approach. The uneven footsteps on the gravel were enough, Alex knew who it was. He held the Glock under the table. The door burst open, and he entered, gun drawn. His eyes upon Alex as soon he entered. He glanced at the papers on the table. Alex looked him over for a few seconds. He was either very confident or considered Alex no threat. 'Nothingman, I assume?' He asked, lowering his gun.

Alex nodded. Said nothing. The cop moved closer and pulled a chair. 'You and me. We are going to have a nice chat. We are going to work something out or you will die. Here. Now. Resisting arrest.' The cop cast his eyes over the rest of the bar.

'If you know who I am. What makes you think I will do anything but kill you.' He looked the cop in the eyes as he spoke. The cop shifted in his seat and tapped his beretta on the table in some sort of warning to Alex. It was futile.

'My employer. The man you seek. Will pay a significant fee to have you leave our organisation alone.' The officer pawed at his belt and pulled a notebook. He scribbled down something, tore off the page and pushed it to Alex.

'Where is Harvey Jupiter?' Alex spoke without breaking eye contact.

'Look at the fucking number on the paper you idiot.' The cop shouted. The pulsing blood vessels on the side of his head looked like living worms under the skin.

'Do you have children? Grandchildren?' Alex asked him. Watching his face redden. His posture tightening up. Nostrils flaring. 'The oath you took, you are a disgrace! Where is Jupiter?' Alex screamed as he swiftly grabbed the officer's gun and slapped him across the face with it. The officer recoiled in the chair as Alex ripped his radio away from him and tossed it to the other end of the room. He stripped the gun and tossed it to the side.

He stood looking at the man. He was soaked in sweat. Clutching his chest. Fumbling at the top button of his shirt as the colour drained from his face. 'Looks like you need a little more help than I'm prepared to give you. Tell me where Harvey Jupiter is, and I'll call an Ambulance.'

'Call it now! So, I know you won't fuck me over.' He shouted as he squirmed in pain. 'I'm dying here! I have drugs in the car, get me to them.'

'You aren't in a position to make demands. You are having a heart attack by the looks of it.' Alex pointed at the paperwork that sat on the table. 'This is unforgivable.' Alex spoke as watched the cop fumble for his cell phone before slapping out of his hand. He stamped on it after it hit the floor.

'He's holed up at the lodge. For fucks sake, take me to my car. Drive me to a hospital. I'll let this slip.' Drenched in sweat. A shade of grey consuming what skin was visible. A blueish tone to his lips, froth forming at the corners of his mouth.

'What lodge?' Alex knew there wasn't much time left for the man, remaining calm.

'Black Lake....' The words barely escaping his lips as he looked to have a seizure. His hands, claw like tight to his chest, eyes rolling, an uncontrollable moan filling the air before he became lifeless. Alex kicked the chair back and the cop hit the floor.

Alex placed a 911 call on the bar tenders cell phone. No words said, just placed it on the bar surface and walked out into the daylight. He got into the car and Misha pulled out and headed in the direction of the resort.

'Jupiter is at Black Lake. A lodge.' He searched the location on his cell as he spoke. 'Could be a setup. Something pre-planned. I need more intel.'

'We could see if Truman can dig anything up. Take some time to get it right.' She spoke nervously, almost afraid to say more. 'If there is a mutual interest then I think it could work.' She sounded tentative, hesitant.

'I don't know what to do next if I'm honest Misha.' He rubbed his forehead, frustrated. 'I feel relief in ridding the world of these bastards but I'm losing myself to the violence. The merciless killing. I ask myself every minute if this is the right thing.' Staring at the roof of the car, he continued. 'In my head I was killing every last one of them, then eating my own gun, if I managed to get that far without dying already.' A tear formed at the corner of his eye, halted from becoming anything by a quick swipe from the back of his hand.

'We can stop. There is enough money to leave and go. South America, The Caribbean, Europe. We can put this hell behind us and disappear.' She had barely convinced herself what she was saying was feasible. The lump in her throat growing, stopping her from saying much more before her emotions burst through.

'You and I both know that is not an option for me. You can go, I am on the hook until it's done. Even then, the VP, Truman, they will have something else for me, until I'm dead or they are.' He took a breath, filling his lungs with air supressing his own emotions.

The buzzing of his cell stopped any reply Misha was formulating. Alex picked up the call. 'Yeah.'

'This is Gina Santos. We need to meet, there are things to discuss.' The voice spoke with confidence. 'Can you meet in an hour, strip mall, same as before?'

'Yeah.' He ended the call. 'Santos, wants to meet at the strip mall. Are you good?' He spoke to Misha as she drove. She nodded and turned off the road at the next exit.

'I'm fine, just feeling overwhelmed I think.' She spoke softly, her words deliberately chosen but meaningful.

Chapter 25

They grabbed a coffee and bagel as they waited for Santos's arrival. 'I'd rather you stayed in the car. I have to insulate you as much as possible. If anything goes wrong, I want to be the only scapegoat. He ran his fingers through her hair and traced along her jawline. 'I need you in a position to vanish if it comes to it.'

'Okay.' She leaned across, kissing him gently. 'I will do whatever you need.'

They left the coffee shop, splitting up, Alex sat on the bench as Misha went back to the car. It wasn't long before Santos parked up and joined him.

'Your friend shot himself, he reached the gun eventually. I'm cleared of the shooting.' She held out a small tablet to him, a video waiting to be played. 'I've kept you out of it. All of it. I plan to release everything I have on the Arc of Evermore in 24 hours.' She placed the tablet in the space between them, she took his hesitance as a positive when he did not take it. 'Do you have anything else for me?'

'Duke's bar was key to their operations. Information on victims. Vulnerable people. All passed from the Police department. They tried to rape a mother in the restroom as her daughter sat waiting for her lunch.' Gritting his teeth at the close of each sentence. 'I've dealt with them, called in a 911. If they disclose what happened and release the information, then we know it's a minority of cops.'

'Duke's is close by; I'll swing by after we are done. Anything on Jupiter?' She studied his face from the side as she waited for his reply.

'A location. Could be a setup.' He hesitated and decided not to give her the potential locus.

'Assuming it's not a setup. Is Harvey Jupiter likely to meet his end?' Santos shifted where she sat. 'You are not being recorded but I want to know when you have finished. I want to be first on scene. This will launch my career to the next level.'

Alex nodded his head in consideration. 'It goes higher than Jupiter, but you will be first to know.' He walked off to the waiting car. Santos Sat for a moment, considering what he had said before making her own exit, heading in the general direction of Dukes in her Prius. She thumbed her cell phone as she walked to the car.

The sound of the car door closing was Misha's cue to begin driving out of the lot. 'What did she want, what happened with Manny?' Her voice uneasy. Her dark eyes registering pain when she said his name.

'Says he managed to get his gun and shoot himself. She's in the clear, probably make a stack on the exclusive interview. She will release everything on The Arc in 24 hours.' He scrolled through his cell phone as he spoke. 'I'll need to move on the lodge. The news release may flush Jupiter out.' He studied a map of the lodge and surrounding area.

'If we are going to hit him on the move, we will need something a little more than our sidearms.' She spoke as Alex nodded his head in agreement.

Chapter 26

They pulled in at a hardware store, Alex checked his pockets and pulled out some cash and the Driver's license assuming the identity of Joel Gray. They entered the store looking like any other normal couple out for some home improvement items. 'Oh, look honey, that marble would look so good in our bathroom. . . that we don't have.' His laughter was followed by Misha's. Three store workers made tactical attempts to accost them as they passed the paint section, kitchen renovation area and the building supply demo area promoting the latest quick set cement. They passed on all offers in a polite manner.

Alex picked up a long blade chainsaw, 50 metres of industrial strength steel cable and tensioner clamps. Misha had a confused look on her face and smiled, she knew Alex would have something already planned and decided she would wait until the application of the plan instead of asking.

'Big project Sir, Ma'am?' The college age kid asked at the checkout. He grinned, flashing a set of braces on each set of teeth. Before Alex could answer Misha decided to have some fun. She read his name from his name badge.

'Well, Reuben, my husband here told me not to drive the truck, but you know, I did. Before I knew it there was a damn tree on the roof. Don't even ask about the Wilson's cat.' She smiled as she wrapped her arm around Alex's. The kid smiled awkwardly, unsure of how to reply and used his scanner to read the bar codes on the items that sat before him. They could see the cogs turning in his head trying to formulate an appropriate reply but instead he just kept smiling.

'Cash or card?' He asked. Alex handed him cash before they gathered the items and left the store. Alex laughed shaking his head as they walked back to the car.

'One road bypasses the lodge where Jupiter is supposed to be, from the satellite mapping it's the only way they can get out, by car.' Alex passed the cell phone that showed the pictures to Misha.

'When?' Was all she asked.

'Tomorrow morning, I will go out and observe the area when it's dark. I'm gonna need to involve Truman for some gear.' He took the cell phone and dialled Ed Truman.

It rang twice before he picked up. 'Brody, what do you need?' Truman asked before he screamed at someone to shut the fuck up, immediately ceasing the background noise. He had a unique way of communication, Alex chuckled to himself.

'I have a location for Jupiter, I'll need access to your hangar for some items.'

'Take what you need. What's our timeline for execution?' He could hear him pulling on a cigar.

'The Arc and their crimes will hit the news tomorrow; I expect it will flush him out of his hole not long after. Needs some recon but I'm moving on it regardless.' Alex altered his route as he drove, towards the hangar at R. R Jackton.

'Have you seen the fucking news?' Truman asked in his own volatile manner. 'That Santos woman is at Dukes bar livestreaming, the can of big, long stinking worms is well and truly open.' Truman laughed.

'You will see something similar tomorrow.' He ended the call. He turned to Misha, 'Check out Santos's livestream, Truman says she's live from Dukes.'

Misha turned up the volume on her cell phone when she found it. Santos spoke of The Arc of Evermore as a cult and set out the bait for her next release. She spoke of Dukes as a key cult site and linked it to various disappearances of young women over the last year. She revealed her own ordeal that took place in a multistorey parking facility where she was shot at, and a man died as a result. Fire, Police and Ambulance operatives could be seen in the backdrop of her report as she ended it.

Alex explained his plan as they drove to the airfield. They were waved through the gate as if they were expected. Truman must have called ahead. Misha showed Alex where the crates that held the guns and other tactical equipment were kept. Alex was unsurprised that they were given free reign over the facility, none of Truman's operatives paid any attention to them.

Alex placed two M4 carbine rifles into a holdall with a few boxes of ammunition. Misha pulled two bulletproof vests from a crate and held them up to Alex. He nodded in approval. He used a crowbar to pop a crate marked explosive. He picked out several M34 grenades, used for signalling and marking areas by the military, they are packed with white phosphorous. Signals and marking were not his intended use, they would burn anything in close range in temperatures over 800 degrees. He placed them in the holdall. 'That's about it, any scopes for night ops?' He asked Misha.

'Yeah, locker at the back there.' She pointed as she stuffed the vests inside another bag. Alex opened the locker and took a spotting scope with night vision capability.

'This is all we need; the rest will be luck and planning.' He lifted the bag and gestured to Misha that it was time to go. She carried a bag as she followed Alex back out to the car.

Alex drove as he spoke to Misha. 'I will go to Black Lake when its dark, observe the place for a few hours, you can stay at the resort and get some rest.' He looked her in the eye. 'I'm gonna need you tomorrow.'

Chapter 27

The lodge sat on the North shore of Black Lake. Alex sat in the dark, hidden in some undergrowth several metres from a silt beach. The water, non-tidal, lapping up to the silt in the ripple effect of some surface disturbance elsewhere. He did not risk a drive by, the road was the separation from the private entrance to the lodge and the man-made beach on the other side. From his position, he observed two large SUV's entering the grounds. The lodge was lit and heavily obscured by the evergreen trees that littered the area. Small electric lantern style lights served either side of the driveway that wound up to the lodge itself, beyond the large iron gates. No foot patrols could be seen, the elevation of the lodge provided a view of the road as it wound around either side of the lake, headlights would be seen of any approaching vehicle in the dark. Alex had parked up at least two miles away and used the cover of the forest to get to his position.

He used the spotting scope and identified an area on the west side that he could easily block the road, the trees were too dense to bypass the road or take an off-road route. Where he had parked his car on the east side was another key location in his plan. He spent another three hours waiting, watching in the darkness. No-one else came or went during this time. Only a few lights stayed on at the lodge as the rest went dark, it looked like whoever was there was in for the night. Alex texted Santos when he got back to the car. He told her to release her information mid-morning and to include that she had received information that Harvey Jupiter was located staying at a lodge in the north of the state. He knew it was risky, she was smart enough to use the process of elimination to figure out where he was, but it was a chance he had to take.

Misha was sat on the couch, wrapped in a blanket drinking hot chocolate when he got back to the resort. He knew she wouldn't have slept knowing he was out there and took comfort in her caring about him. He ran through what he had observed and how his plan would be implemented before they went to bed. They ordered some food from the service menu and streamed a film on the big screen Tv.

Chapter 28

A roadside diner breakfast and coffee was all there was time for before they arrived at Black Lake. A light mist hung over the dark water as it sat still, the surface looked almost solid in its calm. Misha checked the weapons, her own way to channel her pre-op nerves. She adjusted her vest as Alex mounted the cable tensioners at knee height on two trees that sat either side of the road. He would apply the cables later. The trees were around 20 metres apart and he had decided to double the steel cable when it was time. Alex put on his vest and pulled a black hoody on over it. His M4 sat on the passenger seat of the car and his sidearm was holstered to his thigh. The subtle citrus smell of the pine trees filled the air as they ran over the plan, checking they both were on the same page.

The tone that signals breaking news caught their attention as Alex leaned in and turned up the volume of the radio. The newsreader spoke of revelations in the recent events surrounding The Arc of Evermore. Santos had kept her word. The horrific details of the cult, their ideology and actions filled the airwaves. Alex could only imagine what pictures were being shown in the live report on television. Members of The Arc were named and shamed, links to the Police department and how they used officers to identify potential victims was discussed. The voice then stated that Gina Santos would be following up with some big information as Harvey Jupiter had been located at a lodge in the north of the state. That was enough for Alex. He needed no further prompt to get moving.

He grabbed the steel cable and ran it across the road twice in a loop before tensioning it until it sat level at knee height. 'It's time.' He said to Misha as she nodded and hid herself in some bushes.

Alex sped off in the car towards the direction of the lodge. He could imagine the news reaching whoever was in the lodge before it had been announced to the world, he drove at speed, flying past the lodge to the west side where the road narrowed. He performed a U-turn and got out the car in a hurry. The sound of the chainsaw eating through a pine tree filled the surrounding area until a loud crack was heard as the tree trunk broke free and fell, almost in slow motion across the road, bouncing before it came to a stop. His nose was filled with the smell of freshly cut timber before he threw the chainsaw down and ran back to the car. As he opened the door screeching could be heard from the tyres of a vehicle in the distance.

He had barely driven 500 metres before a single blacked out SUV sped past him. There was no chance he could see who was inside. 'Shit!' He shouted as he put down all the windows and sat his rifle across his lap. He kept his eye on the rear-view as the SUV appeared. It was moving fast, gaining on him faster than he would have liked.

The rear window shattered as he saw a muzzle flash in his mirror. The dull sound of bullets hitting the trunk of the car in a short burst was heard before the SUV rear ended him. He fought the steering wheel as the car fishtailed after the impact. He pulled out his sidearm and reached back letting off a few shots of his own. His ears ringing from the sound filling the car. He reached a straight section of road as the SUV lunged closer for a second attempt to ram the car. Alex locked his left arm out straight on the wheel and pivoted his torso round to get a view of the SUV. He held his right arm outstretched, took a deep breath and fired six quick shots into the windscreen where the driver would have been. He watched in the rear-view as the SUV swerved across the road before slowing to a stop.

Chapter 29

Misha had heard the echo of the chainsaw reverberate across from the west side of the lake. It was hard to tell but she thought she could hear a vehicle or vehicles. She had a clear view of the road that led to the where the lodge was. The next noise she heard was the screech of tyres. She turned to see a gunmetal Prius stop at the other side of the steel cable that stretched across the road. It was Gina Santos. Shit, Misha said to herself.

Gina had gotten out of the car, a look of shock on her face that she had nearly driven into the steel cable. Her face contorted further when Misha emerged from where she had hidden, dressed in tactical gear holding an M4. 'Gina, get back in the car!' Misha yelled.

'Where is Harvey Jupiter?' Gina shouted as she walked towards Misha. She tried to project the fiery Latina persona in a futile attempt to conceal her surprise at what she had come across.

'Get the fuck in your car and go, it's not safe here!' Misha barely finished before she heard a vehicle approaching at high speed from the lodge side. As she turned it ploughed straight into the steel cabling. An ear shattering noise filled the air as she ducked, covering her head. The sound of metal screeching as it bent and was contorted by the impact filled the air. The steely twang of the cable rang as a weird chorus. The front of the SUV appeared to eat the cable before flipping on end and coming down hard on to the front of Santos' Prius. Glass.

Plastic and shards of metal flying in all directions. Misha could hear the scream of Santos as the SUV came to rest.

There was some swearing in Spanish. Something about God. She looked up to see Santos standing looking at the wreck in disbelief, shouting at it. 'Move, move, Gina!' Misha shouted as she grabbed her by the arm, pulling her towards the embankment that led to the water, away from the road. Both dead and living pine needles seemed to rain down on them in slow motion as the trees shook.

The sound of car doors closing caused Santos eyes to widen. As Misha turned, she saw Harvey Jupiter and several of his men standing on the road, another SUV stopped in the middle of it. She tried to raise her rifle, but it was too late.

Santos screamed as they opened fire. Misha jerked and stumbled backwards, falling down the embankment. Her rifle landing where Santos stood. Her eyes darted towards where it lay.

'Don't you dare touch that you cunt!' Harvey Jupiter warned. He looked every part the Ivy League graduate Millionaire asshole as he walked towards Gina Santos. The echo of gunshots could be heard in the distance. He looked at her as if he was an apex predator, studying its prey. He grabbed her by the hair and yanked her away from the embankment. A smile cut his face in two as he corralled his victim.

Chapter 30

As Alex neared where he had set the steel cable he saw the taillights of an SUV first, then another SUV on its roof on top of another vehicle. A sudden thump in his chest filled him with dread. His heart slamming against his chest wall with every beat. He pulled the car across the road and jumped out with his M4. A few deep breaths to settle himself. All quiet. The hissing from some steam rising from the upturned cars radiator. Pine needles littered the immediate area, some still fell. He heard nothing else. No-one else. He fumbled for his cell phone, no calls or messages from Misha. He filled his lungs and rounded the car, rifle raised on the SUV, it was empty. He cleared the immediate area, satisfied that no one was hiding. As he approached the cable, he recognised the third vehicle as Santos'. The two occupants of the SUV looked to have died on impact, suspended by their seatbelts upside down. He jumped over the cable and checked the driver's side; she wasn't in the car. His first thought was that Misha had gotten her away then he saw the trouser leg of a pant suit and small foot, toenails painted, outstretched behind the car. What he saw next turned his stomach. The headless body of Gina Santos sat with its back resting on the rear of her car. Her shirt and jacket torn open exposing her breasts, her head sat between her legs, held by her hands, a large hunting knife driven through the top of the skull and a primitive Arc symbol etched into her forehead. It was a statement, a warning.

Alex quickly made his way to the tensioner that anchored the cable. As he loosened the cable something caught his eye in his peripheral vision. His stomach knotted, his mouth filled with saliva and his chest becoming tight as he saw Misha laying at the water's edge. He felt sick.

He scrambled down the embankment to where she lay. His eyes fixated on her, looking for movement. Looking for a clue as to what had happened. The back of her head sitting in the shallow water, clouds of blood bobbing back and forth with the ripples. He could see two bullet holes on her chest. A mixture of mud and blood on the left side of her face.

'Misha! Hey! Hey!' He shouted as he got closer. A quiet snoring sound could be heard, shallow rise and fall of her chest could be seen. He checked her airway, no blood, it was clear. He unzipped her jacket and saw the deformed metal slugs embedded in the vest she wore. He ripped off the Velcro and tossed the vest aside. Her breathing was less restricted. He ran his hands over her head and felt a bump on the back of it, his hand covered in her blood from a wound. He wiped away some of the mud on her face to reveal some scratches and abrasions.

Adrenaline was pumping hard, he managed to get her up over his shoulder and carry her up to the car. He used his hand to wipe off the glass from the rear window before placing her down on her side. She made some incomprehensible noises, a good sign, he thought. He ran back down and grabbed her vest to avoid her DNA being traced. Her blood was in the Lake; they wouldn't be able to use it. After fighting hard to remove the cable and tensioners he returned to the car.

He bandaged Misha's head using a dressing from the first aid kit from that was in the trunk. He lifted her shirt and checked under her sports bra, she was already badly bruised above her right breast and on her sternum from the gunshot trauma. A million thoughts raced through his head, at the top of the list, was Misha, and who he could get help from, fuck Jupiter, she needs me, he surmised.

As he started driving away from the wreck, he thought he heard something, the wind coming in through the broken window distorted it, his ears rang from the shooting inside the car. 'Alex'. It was Misha, he slowed down and turned to see her. She vomited on the floor of the car. Some it clung to her hair.

'Just sit tight, you are hurt, I'm gonna get you some help.' The concern in his voice evident.

'My ribs are broken. My head..' She wiped the strings of saliva off her mouth with her hand. She looked like she would vomit again.

'It's okay, just relax, I'm gonna have to take you to Truman.' Speaking as he slowed the car and reached back, holding her hand.

'Gina. I told her.' A grimace filtering across her face as she spoke. 'Harv... Jupiter, he got me, before I.'

Alex could not believe what he saw ahead of him. A very well-dressed man standing by the edge of the road. It was Harvey Jupiter, holding his hand out as to stop a passing motorist. He spoke firmly to Misha. 'I need you to hold on.' The engine getting louder as his foot pushed closer to the floor.

Jupiter wore a disarming smile on his face, he stood at the side of the road by a derelict ranger station. Alex had reached his desired speed. Harvey Jupiter's facial expression did not change until Alex was close enough that his anger and hatred could be seen. He swerved into Jupiter instead of stopping. The loud thud as Harvey Jupiter rolled up the wing of the car and off the roof was satisfying. Alex could see him laying by the road in a heap for a few seconds before three armed men ran out from the ranger satiation and dragged him away, letting off a few shots from a pistol in Alex's direction. He was grateful an innocent motorist hadn't passed before he did, they would have been ambushed by his goons.

Alex stopped the car a hundred metres or so along the road. He grabbed his rifle, two spare magazines and an M34 grenade. 'I got him, Misha, I'll end this scumbag right here.' He pushed a section of matted hair off her face before getting out of the car.

He walked up the middle of the road, rifle traced on the ranger station, he knew they could see him, they hadn't the range to hit him with any deadly force with their arsenal. He heard the crunching of dead pine needles off to the right, someone was trying to flank him from the cover of the trees. He let off three shots as he heard the crunching stop. A yelp. Heavy breathing. A hit. A man lay on his back with a sucking chest wound a few metres into the treeline. He shot him in the face when he found him. Alex stayed in the treeline as he got closer to where his target was hiding. He stopped dead around 20 metres from it as he heard another of The Arc's men trying to be silent. The problem with trying to stay silent is that they are too tense, rigid, with poor weight distribution. He came into Alex's view; he held a pistol as he crept from the blindside of the shack. Pop. Pop. Two shots dropped him where he stood.

'Alright Nothingman! We get the point. Only one of us has a weapon in here.' A muffled cough. 'We will throw it out, we pose no danger. You, and I, need to talk.'

The ranger station was constructed on thin slatted timber. Mostly rotted. A few slats missing. He could hear the muffled coughs, they were lower. Jupiter must be hurt enough to be laying down, he thought. He flicked full auto on his M4 before aiming at what would be the average man's chest height. He pushed in a full mag of 30 rounds and emptied them across the shack. The sound echoed across the entire area and would be heard miles away. 'Fuuuuuuccckckkkkk!' Jupiter screamed.

Alex kicked the flimsy door off the hinges. It skidded along the floor to within inches of where Harvey Jupiter sat shaking. His bodyguard lay oozing blood across his legs, pinning him. His sand-coloured suit, torn, marked with mud from where Alex had used the car to hit him. His left foot pointed at an unnatural angle, blood soaked through his sock.

Harvey Jupiter held his hands up as he spoke. One hand sat at an unnatural angle from his wrist. It also must have been smashed by the impact of the car. 'Let's talk. Surely you want something? Why have you come for us?'

'You are an abomination. Using innocent people in a psychotic pursuit of something that does not exist!' Alex bellowed in the small shack.

'You are mistaken, the blood of the young nourishes our elders, our land, it is for a better future, longer life!' He spat as he spoke. He appeared to believe the words. A passion across his face.

'Who is the head of the snake? Who are you fronting for?' Alex moved closer, reloading the M4.

'Tell me why you want to know? Tell me why you are doing this, Nothingman!'

'You killed my family. My wife. My child. The 33rd street car bombing.' Alex seethed with sheer venom. It emanated towards Jupiter.

'You are mistaken. Idiot.' Harvey Jupiter laughed.

Alex let off another round into the man who lay across Harvey Jupiter's legs. Jupiter yelped in fear. 'We are not responsible for that! We did not sanction the bombing! You are being manipulated, played like a little toy!'

'Your insignia was carved into their flesh.' Alex shouted at him, enraged.

'You are a fucking fool. A woman and child would be a waste of resource. Think about it.' The horrible grin on his face was enough for Alex, this man and everything he stood for disgusted him. He shot him through the hand.

After the screaming, Jupiter spoke again, snot running down into his mouth, his eyes filling with tears. 'My boss is untouchable. He is the next President you fucking animal! The tears of Jupiter programme is his, borne of his vision! I am a face, nothing more, to protect the establishment! I'm expendable, like you!'

Alex shot him in the other hand. 'A name! Give me a fucking name.'

'Terrence fucking Enoch! Please! Stop!' Harvey Jupiter screamed.

'You are an intelligent man Harvey; do you know what white phosphorous does to human flesh?' He pulled the pin from the M34 grenade and tossed it onto Harvey Jupiter's lap as he walked out. Misha was first to his thoughts as he started to jog back down the road to the car. The bang filling the air was all Alex needed. Behind him the shack burned in a white cloud. If there was a scream, it couldn't be heard.

He could see Misha sat upright in the back of the car as he approached. Her hand reaching up to feel the back of her bandaged head.

'Hey, how are you?' He asked as he jumped in the car. 'Let's get you some help.' Pulling back on to the road.

'Let's just go back to the resort. I'm banged up is all. They won't do anything for my ribs, you know.' She winced between every sentence. 'Besides, I've had worse.'

'Oh yeah?' He asked, wondering if she had been shot before. He didn't recall any stories of her being shot or roughed up this bad.

'Yeah, some guy hit me with a hammer and broke my arm.' Her laugh turned into a moan as she clutched her chest.

Alex smiled at her through the rear-view mirror. 'We need to ditch this car. The new ventilation isn't what I paid for.'

'The hangar.' She used her cell phone camera to check her face, wiping the dirt away with a wet wipe from the car. 'Ed has plenty others we can use.'

Alex dialled Truman's number on his cell and placed it on speaker. It was several rings before he picked up. 'Ed. Jupiter is down. I need a vehicle and some medical supplies.'

'I saw the news, is she gonna release any more?' Truman sounded serious. Clearly needing an answer before moving on.

'The news will have something but not what you think.' Alex looked at Misha in the back before he continued. 'Harvey Jupiter beheaded Santos before I caught up with him. Carved an Arc symbol in her forehead. That'll be the news.' He saw a sadness wash over Misha as he told him about Santos.

'For fucks sake! I'm at the hangar, come by, what do you want? SUV? Sedan?' Truman sounded disgusted. He ended the call from his end.

Alex drove the route carefully, avoiding attention and avoiding any bumps in the road. He could tell every time a bump or turn in the road caused Misha more pain in the back of the car. Her face hid nothing.

Truman paced back and forth along the large aircraft entrance of the hangar, hand waving between gesturing to whomever he was on the phone to and puffing a cigar. Alex noted that he looked animated. Wondering who he had been calling. His first thought was the Vice President. There was no way to tell. As soon as Truman saw the car pulling in at the hangar he ended the call, waving them inside.

Truman walked to the car, craning his neck to look into the back. 'What the fuck happened to her?' He turned and shouted something that drew a familiar face out of the office. Alex got out the car and rushed to the back, helping Misha out of the rear of the vehicle. The weasel looking Dr Clark scurried towards them. An uncomfortable expression dressed his face.

'Oh dear, what happened to her Mr Brody?' He asked, using his hand to hurry them as he retreated backwards towards the office.

'Head trauma, two gunshots to the chest, she was wearing a vest.' Alex said, concern in his voice as he and Truman took an arm each to support Misha as she struggled toward the office.

Clark was examining Misha and her wounds in the office. Alex and Truman sat on some small crates outside as Truman's men did whatever they did in the hangar, moving boxes, filling out itinerary sheets, planning dawn raids on small South American country.

'Do you know who it is on Capitol Hill?' Truman asked direct, straight to the point. 'He will want to know.'

'Terrence Enoch. Will that come as a shock?' Alex asked.

'No.' Truman lit another cigar and poured a bourbon for them both. 'He will be hard to get at. He say anything else?'

'Yeah, he reckoned you played me. The 33rd street bombing that took Sarah and Emily wasn't The Arc and that you used it as motivation for your Nothingman.' Alex looked for a flinch, a change in posture, anything. He had had suspicions over The Arc, Truman, everything, and had shown his cards to Truman.

'How much will you believe in what I tell you?' Truman stared him right in the eye.

Before Alex could answer, Clark spoke. 'Your friend is resting; I have given a mild sedative and some pain relief. There are a few broken ribs and potential for a minor concussion. I have stapled the wound to her head. She needs some rest for a few days.' He moved closer. 'Any more headaches Mr Brody?'

'No, not like before, only after too much bourbon.' Alex sensed Truman tighten up as he spoke to Clark.

'Good.' He smiled before Truman swung around and shot him in the head. The gunshot from the revolver breaking the silence in the hangar. Clark dropped exactly where he had stood. Dead. In a heap.

'Fucking rat!' Truman shouted. 'That piece of shit was in the process of selling you to the south Americans, apparently he can replicate the fucking serum!'

'What!?' Alex stared at Truman. 'Are you serious?'

'Yeah. That call. My counterpart in the operations south of Mexico met with this shit faced rat.' He sipped his bourbon. 'Claimed he could get you out in the open and they would snatch you. To make himself rich, off you!'

'Who else knows about me?' Alex looked at the expanding pool of blood that surrounded Clark's head as he asked Truman.

'Me and our friend in the white house.' Truman did not delay, it sounded believable. 'Now, you are right. Sarah and Emily were not targets of The Arc. Two scumbag fuckers trying to join them did it. They were refused entry as they were too radical, too noticeable, white supremacist ties. Based on our intel.' Truman topped up his glass before speaking again. 'I embellished their connection thinking it would provide some drive for you.' He looked Alex in the eye as he spoke. 'They did it to get noticed by The Arc, not for The Arc.'

Alex shook his head. 'It wouldn't change what I have done. If you told me what The Arc did to women and children, I'd have killed them anyway.'

Truman looked relieved; he had expected Alex to strike him at least. He nodded towards the office before speaking again. 'I was wrong about her. One tough fucking broad. Take the Lincoln. Get your head down for a few days. Things will go nuclear if what you said about Santos and Jupiter hits the ten o'clock.'

Alex got up and walked to the office, stepping over the body of Clark. Misha lay in a sedated state, face cleaned up, smaller cuts on her hands dressed and a bottle of painkillers sat next to her. 'Help me get her in the car.'

Truman and Alex carried Misha to the car and sat her in the passenger seat before reclining it. Truman spoke as Alex started up the motor. 'The next one is the hardest part of this thing; I'll speak to our friend to see how he wants it to go down.' He closed the door and tapped it twice as he walked back toward the office.

Chapter 30

He drove back to the resort. Radio off, listening to the deep, regular rhythm of her breathing. Consumed by a heavy guilt that she lay there, sedated, having been shot twice and could have died, all because she was involved with him. He promised himself, promised her, that he would finish this himself and keep her safe. She had done enough.

He noticed a bag sat in the footwell, between Misha's feet. He slowed the vehicle as he reached down and grabbed it, pulling it up on to his lap. It was full of cash. Easily another twenty grand in mixed notes.

The resort looked beautiful in the contrast of darkness and strategically placed uplighters. Like a fairy-tale village in some alpine setting. He got the car as close as he could, waiting until an older couple were out of sight before scooping up Misha and carrying her into their lodge. She mumbled something he did not understand in her sedated state as he placed her on the bed. He got what remained of her clothing off and dressed her in her oversized Led Zeppelin t shirt and a pair of his own boxer shorts. After placing a few bottles of water and the pain pills on the bedside cabinet, he poured himself a large measure of the bourbon that sat on the kitchen counter.

He switched on the Tv and selected the news channel from the menu. The headline bar read Gina Santos murdered by The Arc of Evermore. Hero reporter dies in the line of duty exposing the worst cult since that of Charles Manson in the late 60's. The news reader shed a false tear as he explained how Gina Santos was mutilated and marked by the cult insignia, the body of cult leader Harvey Jupiter was found nearby, burned to death after suffering multiple gunshot wounds. A local man gave interview with the burnt-out ranger station in the background. He explained how he had found several dead men leading up to the burning structure that morning.

Alex channel surfed through half the list and the Santos-Jupiter story dominated every news channel and he decided to turn off the Tv.

The old familiar burn of bourbon taking the path of least resistance towards his throat was a feeling he appreciated after what had happened. His cell phone buzzed in his pocket. He considered just letting it ring out. They would leave a message if it was important or relevant. No caller ID, the display read. He answered and decided not to speak. He just listened.

'Nothingman.' A pause. A voice he did not recognise. 'You are becoming a huge inconvenience.' Another pause. 'I do not take kindly to such things.' The voice was that of an educated man. Someone that was used to having their own way. Alex could imagine someone on the other end foaming at the mouth, staring at the phone as their knuckles were white as they gripped it, ready to spout pure venom at any moment of weakness. 'You will talk to me. You will be interested in what I have to say.'

Alex decided to end the call. Testing the resolve of the mystery caller. He wondered if another key player was now ready to introduce themselves. The cell phone buzzed again. He accepted the call and said nothing.

'I will ask that you cease and desist in your campaign of violence and futility against The Arc of Evermore. This is the only time that I will ask. A courtesy that some feel you should not be extended.'

Alex took another sip of his bourbon. 'Well. You know who I am. Who might you be?' Alex added his own pause. 'Do you know why I do what I do. Do you know what it will take for me to stop?'

'My name is Carl Cooper. My employer is, let's say invested in something you seek to destroy. You do what you do because you are a sheep. Someone barks and you go and do what they want you to.' Another baited pause. 'Ed Truman will meet his end. He has used you. If you are as effective and as ruthless as you are billed to be, my guess is that you will stop when I remove your spine from your body.' Alex could tell the caller had moved during the conversation, ambient noise, outside, somewhere open. 'We could use a man of your skill set or we could make you live a very comfortable life, never have to work again in a place of your choosing.'

'Carl. If that is your name.' Alex mimicked the pause his adversary had been using between sentences. 'How about you tell your employer, the nice comfortable life he enjoys, the money he enjoys, the little band of yes men that he has on the hook are all going to disappear. I will play a key part in ending The Arc of Evermore and Terrence Enoch.' Alex felt he played his card too soon; they might not have known he knew the head of the snake was Enoch.

Incessant forced laughter poured from the speaker of Alex's cell phone. 'I do not know if you understand how happy that makes me Nothingman.' The laugher continued. 'I will really enjoy coming to that little resort you are sitting in, those lodges do look beautiful, that panoramic view through those big windows. Not a bad final view I'd say.' He paused, he knew he had Alex where he wanted him, Alex felt the burst of adrenaline as it was pumped around his body. The fight or flight response was in full flow. 'I think that you will benefit from watching what I do to Ed Truman first, I have plans for him, and bigger plans for you.' The line went dead. Silent.

Alex quickly scrambled, turning off the lights, he could see the outside better now it was no longer obscured by the internal lights returning his own reflection. He knew it was only a matter of time when someone discovered where they were staying. The threat seemed too calm, too calculated, designed to cause him alarm and unease, to make him uncomfortable. It would be a huge and potentially deadly gamble if they stayed put. Equally as huge if he made a snap decision to move, they'd be vulnerable on the road leaving the resort, an easy target. He rationalised, if someone was outside with a bead on him, he was a very easy target sat watching the news or stood on the cell phone. He decided to leave every external light on, secured every window, door and headed to the bedroom.

Misha lay in bed, still as he had placed her. Her breathing a deep, regular almost machine-like pattern. There were no nearby structures that would allow a potential attacker any view into the bedroom. He decided they would move at first light. He was conflicted, thinking about calling Truman, letting him know this Carl character had named him, threatened his life. He dialled Trumans number and stepped into the bathroom, closing the door. Two rings. Voicemail. He didn't leave a message and tried again. Two rings and voicemail again. Alex was irritated at the thought Truman was screening his calls. He took a quick shower and climbed into bed, trying not to disturb Misha.

It felt like his eyes had closed for twenty seconds before Emily came to him, bleeding, burned and screaming for him. He woke, catching his rapid breathing, coaching it to slow. He managed some more light sleep before the alarm on his cell woke him. He had set it for 0500am. His head played out potential scenarios most of the night, it was a poor recipe for someone needing some genuine rest. He had thought about taking a drive past Manny's place, see if it was an option to hide out, he ruled it out quickly, there would have been a search and seizure following his death. He thought about the Silent knight, Truman's hangar and even Earl's cabin. He packed their clothes, food and arms quickly, it reminded him of the rapid upheaval he had experienced when on deployment overseas. It wasn't uncommon for his squad to have to move whenever intel was received about the enemy. It was the first time he thought that it was reasonable, even feasible to run. Head out of the states.

Misha had stirred a few times during the night, used the bathroom, winced with the pain when she moved suddenly, Alex heard everything, noticed everything.

'They know where we are, don't they?' She spoke as he zipped up a holdall.

'I got a call. Last night. They seemed to know where we are. Made a threat.' He stopped and looked over to where she was perched on the edge of the bed. 'How are you feeling?'

'Better. My ribs hurt. The head isn't so bad. What did they say?'

'The guy reckons he will get to Truman first. Then me. Described the resort and the cabin.' He slid the holdall along the polished floor towards the doorway.

'What ae you thinking? A viable threat?'

'Yes. A lot of ego. Some madness in the voice, the way he projected himself. I think it's serious, I think he's confident enough to tell me his plan as he has the means to enact it.'

'Will you tell Ed?'

'I tried last night. Screened the calls, a couple of rings and voicemail.' Alex swept up the car keys from the bedside table.

'...And he hasn't replied, you haven't missed a call?' Confusion marked her face, suspicion in the tone and inflection of her voice.

'You find that unusual?' He picked up her bag and headed toward the door. 'You know him better than I do, what are you thinking?'

'Well, he tends to be a control freak, where his interests are directly affected. I'd say you are his primary interest at this point.' She moved in a rigid fashion, protecting her injuries, a subconscious effort to avoid that sharp pain inhibiting her breathing. Alex considered what she had said as he heard the shower running as he took their bags downstairs.

He sat with a coffee whilst he waited for Misha to get ready. Another helping sat in the cafetiere, he hoped she would take it to go, he felt an anxious cloud descend as he waited.

Chapter 31

Misha looked a better colour as she sat in the passenger seat. Alex had no idea where they would be going but he knew he had to think outside the box, things had changed. His cell buzzed. Truman's caller ID lit up the screen. Alex answered and flicked on speakerphone.

'Yeah, Truman, we need to talk.' The urgency evident in his voice.

'Yes we do.' Truman paused. 'Remember that tracking device I put in your daughter's pendant?' Alex and Misha both looked at each other, no words were needed between them. Something was wrong.

'I do.'

'Well, it clogged my fucking drain, my home insurance won't cover the work.' Truman said before a fleshy thud was heard. A short silence occupied the line.

'I know not what you and this degenerate get up to in each other's homes, but I have had enough.' That aura of consummate confidence, arrogance, Carl Cooper's voice, instantly recognisable. 'Your terminus is close Nothingman, Old Ed here, well, he is about to find out the lengths that I will go to in order to satisfy my employer.' The call ended from the other end.

'What the hell was Ed on about?' Misha asked, her brow furrowed.

Alex put his foot down, the motor running harder. 'The airfield, he was letting me know where he is.'

'Alex, they could be working together, have you given that a thought.'

'Either way, this guy is something that I need to deal with, his type does not stop, they keep coming.' His eyes staring a hole in the road ahead, pure focus, his mind was made up. 'You need to sit this one out, you have had enough, I will drop you at the Silent Knight.'

'No.' The atmosphere in the vehicle could be cut with a knife. 'Not an option' She winced as she pulled a holdall from the backseat and pulled out Alex's rifle, checking the ammo and breech. The noise as she pulled apart the Velcro of his vest contested the droning of the motor as it ate up the road ahead. She popped off his seatbelt and manoeuvred the vest into position on his torso, securing it with the Velcro. There was no need for any words. He understood her conviction, her investment, and the potential sacrifice she was about to make.

Alex slowed the car at the gate to the airfield, the guard at the gate sat on his chair with his head extended backwards. A grotesque wound across his neck showed a severed Trachea. The hangar was no different looking to the last visit, roller door closed two vehicles parked up outside. As the distance closed between Alex and the hangar, a figure appeared from the doorway and held his rifle trained on Alex as he approached.

The man held his hand up, telling Alex to stop. He considered putting the foot down and running into the man. Instead, he decided to play ball, parking the car where he was indicated.

'Switch the motor off and get out!' A fair-haired mercenary type screamed. A south African accent, Alex thought, recognising the inflection of the man's words. He did as the man demanded. Alex exited the vehicle, the vest felt tight around his torso, a loose-fitting hoodie concealed it. His M4 was grasped in one hand. He could rush the man and be upon him in half a dozen strides. High chance the man would get a shot off if he was trained half as well as his appearance suggested. The man's eyes darted to the rifle as Alex rounded the vehicle. 'Put that fucking thing down!'

'If I was going to use it, you'd be dead already.' Alex smiled, sensing the apprehension and something else in the man. Was it fear, had the legend of the Nothingman reached this piece of meat as he stood, waiting to be cut down. Alex decided to toy with him, hoping he would focus on him and stay focused on him. He kept his gun in his hand.

'Right! You are fucking dead if you breathe wrong ey! Get inside, stay in front of me uh.' A change in the voice, hesitance. Confirming Alex's perception, fear. South African, the rolling of the letter r and how he closed his conversation confirmed Alex's guess.

Alex slowly walked through the door, holding the door for the man, who would not move any closer. 'Just go, move, leave the door uh!' He let the door go and headed inside the hangar. The irregularity of the man's boots meeting the concrete floor behind him told Alex that the man was out of his depth, he stumbled trying to keep his gun trained on Alex and negotiating the doorway in fear of what Alex would do in such proximity. 'Sir! I've got the Nothingman!' He shouted. Alex could see movement in Truman's office. The door opened; the squeak of the hinges echoed through the hangar. 'You are in trouble now eh boy!' The man was irritating. His attempt to try and scare Alex wore thin very quickly. The sound of a wheeled office chair cascading over the concrete flooring kept Alex's attention on the office.

Ed Truman appeared in the doorway. Bound to the chair. He was being pushed out into the open by two other men. They were also dressed like the idiot who had now moved around to Alex's left side. Ed's chin was resting on his thick chest. His amber tint glassed still rested on his nose. The thinned-out hair on top more obvious in the bright white light, his head tilted in such a way a polished shine could be seen where light meets scalp. Dark, dried blood had been deposited on his bowling shirt at some point.

The voice of Carl Cooper boomed from behind Truman as the two goons parted. 'Well. Here we are.' He walked out behind Truman. He stood around six two, he was lean, completely bald with a nose that dominated is face. It was off centre and characterised with a pronounced bump where it had been broken, probably a few times. He carried the sand-coloured field jacket Truman had worn previously; his index finger outstretched on the wire coat hanger. A nickel-plated pistol in his right hand. 'I trust that you have no issues hearing Nothingman.' He smiled a false, morbid smile. It revealed near perfect teeth, but his front right incisor was snapped off at an angle. 'I am sure Mr Du Plessis requested that you leave your guns outside, no?'

'Yeah, he did.' Alex stared through Carl Cooper. His peripheral vision picking up the movement of Du Plessis. If straight ahead represented 12 on a clock face, he stood around the 10 o'clock position, nervous, swaying on the spot. 'I had another idea, if I am honest.' As Alex spoke the last words in that sentence, he casually raised his M4 across his body and squeezed the trigger. A shot rang out in the hangar and Du Plessis dropped to the floor like a puppet having had its strings snipped. Alex kept his eyes on Cooper. No reaction. No blinking of the eyes. No shifting of weight in readiness to take cover. Instead, he raised his weapon as quick as a flash, discharging two shots.

Alex dropped to his knees, gasping for breath. It felt like he had been hit by a sledgehammer. His eyes watered as he fought for a breath. The two goons rushed him kicking away his rifle and taking away his pistol. His knee burned with the friction against the concrete as they dragged him closer to Truman and Cooper.

'I am so happy you wore a vest!' Cooper laughed a false laugh. The joy on his face made Alex's skin crawl.

A hand grabbed Alex's hair, pulling his head upwards until he was up on his knees. 'Stay there.' A voice spoke before two sets of footsteps headed back towards the door he had come through.

'You are going to watch old Ed here, suffer, suffer some more, and die today.' Cooper removed Trumans jacket from the wire hangar and dropped it to the floor. He paced a few steps either side of Truman as he unwrapped the coat hanger, leaving the hook end as intended. 'I always thought his glasses were a bit, 1980's, ever seen that move with Al Pacino and Johnny Depp? You know, the mafia one, old school mob guy, amber tinted glasses, fur coat?'

Alex didn't speak, he wasn't sure he would manage a full response without gasping for air as he tried to recover from the blunt force trauma to his chest. He watched Cooper use what hair was left on Trumans head to yank his head back. Truman groaned as he was stimulated into regaining consciousness.

Truman looked at Alex, his eyes said what his words would have had Cooper not punched him in the mouth before he spoke a word. 'You have been permitted to operate Ed, that permission is now revoked, you are old news, and it is time to pay the price for the things you have set in motion. Cooper stood side on as he spoke to Truman before turning his head, a maniacal grin flashing those teeth again as he used the coat hanger and stabbed Truman in the left eye, twisting and yanking it out as a combination of Truman screaming and Cooper laughing filled the hangar with a chaotic noise. Blood ran from his eye giving Trumans face an odd half painted look as he squirmed in the chair and went limp.

Cooper was still laughing; he performed a weird two step shuffle as he circled Truman. 'Next, I will take his balls!' His laughter was sickening. He leaned in and used Trumans chin to tilt his head up, admiring his handiwork.

The door of the hangar banged twice. Cooper turned, his gaze beyond Alex. The lines on his forehead showing an aspect of confusion or surprise.

'Psssssst.' It was Truman. Cooper snapped his head back around to face Truman. Truman leaned forward, mouth open and latched on to Cooper's nose, tearing like a rabid dog, it was Cooper's turn to scream.

Cooper pulled away, falling to ground as his gun slid across the floor, a trail of blood formed between Truman and where Cooper scrambled away. Truman spat some tissue out on to the floor and smiled, showing his bloody teeth. The door burst open, and Alex turned as he got to his feet. He Saw Misha burst through the door, pistol raised, three shots rang out. The muzzle flash was less than a metre from the first man as his face exploded launching a red-pink mist into the air. She turned and took aim at the second. Click. Click. The gun had jammed. She threw the gun at the man's head like a baseball pitcher as he rushed towards her. She was far too prepared for him as she turned her body, thrusting her hip into his upper leg, pulling his lead arm into her chest as he went head over heels crashing to the concrete. Before he could even make an attempt to get up, she delivered three quick punches to his throat.

The gasping sound was a mixture of air and fluid as he rolled and began to crawl away from her. She flicked her hair out of her eyes and followed him. Wearing a look on her face that betrayed any pain she felt from her injuries. Her left hand grabbed a clump of his hair as she drove the blade of a knife through the base of his skull. A second or two was enough to stop all twitching as he lay face down in a puddle of his own blood.

Alex rushed towards Truman and untied the ligature that held him to the chair. Cooper was gone. A trail formed by droplets of blood lead to the fire exit. He glanced quickly at Misha and then to Truman.

'Go kill that fucking freak!' Trumans voice was strained as the sound of screeching tyres was heard outside.

Alex sprinted as he loosened the bulletproof vest, easing the pressure he felt on his chest. Through the fire exit, rounding the building to where he saw a car speeding away, towards the gate of the airfield. He knew it was futile to give chase.

Misha was ripping open a dressing from a first aid kit as she stood in front of Truman. Alex watched as she placed some gauze over his eye and wrapped the dressing in an off-kilter fashion to place pressure over what remained of his eye. The grimace on his face. The beads of sweat littering his forehead, he was suffering, and Alex assumed the eye was lost.

Alex said nothing, he only watched what happened next, finding it odd and amusing at the same time. Truman put his amber tint glasses back on, over his good eye and the one patched up and bleeding, as if there was no reason not to.

'Think you could take me somewhere I can get this fixed up?' Truman spat on a silk handkerchief he pulled from a pocket. 'Thing is, its fucked. I know that but I'd rather not die from the fucking infection.' He rubbed his cheek and his nose in an attempt to clean up the blood. He began to laugh as he tilted his head, looking at the bloody flesh on the floor. 'Oh shit, I got a little more than I thought!'

'I'll catch up with him.' Alex spoke as he looked away from the piece of nose on the floor. 'You got a medical contact we can get you to?'

'Yeah. I'll give you the directions.' Truman walked into the office and returned with a bottle of bourbon. Taking several large gulps of it before offering it to Alex and Misha. They both decided against it.

Truman made a call that explained detailed instructions to someone to get the hangar cleaned and retuned to whatever standard he demanded. The drive was less than a half hour. A nice, well maintained residential area was where they ended up, he was insistent on Alex and Misha going inside with him as they parked up outside a nice-looking house. Alex refused but instead offered a compromise that they'd wait in the car.

'Fine. Give me an hour.' Truman said as he got out of the car with his bourbon. They both watched him as he banged on the door, and it was answered by a woman. She looked around a similar age to Truman. She ushered him inside, a look of shock on her face could be seen and she closed the door.

Alex reclined his seat a little as they waited. 'That was pretty slick back there. Truman was dog meat had you not burst in when you did.'

'It took me long enough to get out the trunk without screaming with these ribs.' Misha looked down her top, checking out the progression of the bruising. 'That damn gun, I've never had one jam like that!'

'You should have used those skills when I met you in Manny's kitchen.' Alex smirked. 'Could have avoided all this madness.' He laughed and checked himself, reminded of the pain across his chest. Misha looked at him, an exaggerated look on her face telling him she was not amused with his attempt at humour.

Alex turned up the heat and decided he would close his eyes, get some rest. His cell phone buzzed, destroying any chance of resting whilst Truman was away. He picked up the call.

'Mr Brody, this line is encrypted and cannot be traced, recorded or used in any attempt to reveal what is discussed. I trust that you know who I am.' The deep voice of Marcus Hall was easily recognisable. 'I cannot seem to reach our friend from the hangar, I need you both to come in.'

'Our friend ran into some difficulty. At this moment, he is on the end of some medical help.' Alex flicked it on to loudspeaker, for the benefit of Misha.

'That statement could have several meanings Mr Brody. I hope that you both have been playing nice.'

'Indeed. A third party from another mutual interest of ours managed to get close.'

A deep exhalation on Marcus' end. 'Tell him to call me. This cannot wait!' The line went dead.

Alex let out a sigh. His eyes met Misha's as he got out the car, no words needed. He walked up to the house and banged on the door. It was several minutes before the woman answered, a look of disdain displayed on her face. She clearly did not appreciate the interruption. 'You are with Edmund, yes?' She spoke with an eastern European accent. Alex nodded and she ushered him inside, casting her eyes over him.

The home was immaculate inside, tiled floors throughout the ground level. He noticed a chemical smell in the air as the woman walked a few paces ahead of him. Several framed certificates from educational providers littered the wall on his right-hand side. A quick glance told him her name was Karyna Lupienski, Doctor in neurological science and surgery. It did not surprise Alex that Truman had such contacts. Instead, it was the photo he set eyes upon, sat in a well laid out snug, on a cabinet next to a chesterfield style chair. It showed the woman and Ed Truman in what looked like a vacation photo. Both looked younger. They continued down the hallway, through an open plan style kitchen and into a brightly lit room sat just off to the side.

Truman was reclined in a chair, like that of a dentist's, his head clamped in. Chopin played on an early model iPod sat in a docking station. The woman used a rub on her hands before she put on gloves. A tray of syringes, bloody swabs and other surgical tools sat in close by. 'Edmund, you have a visitor.' The woman spoke as she moved a magnifier across the area between her face and his.

'Let me guess Brody. The VP needs us?' His words slurring and augmented by the restriction of the clamps. 'Fucking cell hasn't stopped buzzing since that weird motherfucker got to me.'

Alex noticed that Trumans good eye was patched as the other was worked upon. 'Yeah, I have a bad feeling about it Ed.'

Truman waved his right hand in the air. 'Do me a favour Brody. Grab my bottle and gimme a little fucking pour.' He opened his mouth as much as the clamps allowed.

'Edmund! Do not make this more difficult than it is!' The woman scolded him. 'You will have vision of only one eye, I will make it so that you have no vision on the other! Behave!'

'He wants you to call in, I'm going back to the car. Call me when you are ready to go, I'm going to grab a coffee and something to eat.' Alex left the room and retraced his steps to leave the house.

Chapter 32

A lex and Misha sat in a nearby café. Before them sat some coffees and pastrami, cheese and pickle bagels. 'Things are about to get worse; I can't assume that madman running free after Truman taking his nose off won't come back on us. He has seen you now. You will be a target.' He dropped a sugar cube into his coffee.

'Yeah, wouldn't be an issue if my gun hadn't jammed. I'd have shot him too.' She started blankly out the window as she spoke.

Alex watched her and wondered if there was a point up until now that she wished she had never started on this journey. She had to know by now that any future that involved them both would never be normal. He would be on the hook to the Vice President and Ed Truman for as long as he lived. There was another option and Alex would be lying if it hadn't crossed his mind. He could take actions to ensure both men didn't have a pulse. The idea of that very thought caused Alex an internal distress. He thought about how far he come, how easy it was for him to enact violence and outright murder in the name of revenge. He was willing to go to a place most men only saw in a movie or thought about in a fit of rage, despair or anger. That day Truman ordered the good doctor to proceed with putting the nanomachines into his bloodstream really was the day Alex Brody had become less human. Being told a cult had murdered the only people who mattered to him officially locked the pressure valve. He knew he would have to be killed in order to stop. Was it possible for a man of violence, a man of war to become human again? Even after enacting so much upon his fellow human being. His thoughts were interrupted by Misha nudging his plate towards him. He hadn't heard what she said but it would have been a push for him to eat, he assumed.

He took a few bites of his food and sipped his coffee. His thoughts became focused on the next play. Sending Misha away would not go down well, with her at least. Could he end Truman and the VP once he knew she was gone. He asked himself why the VP was calling them in. 'I don't think I can involve you in what comes next.' Speaking as he looked at her, dabbing some mustard from the corner of her mouth. Her eyebrows telling him exactly what she thought of it before she even spoke. 'The VP doesn't know you, your level of involvement, I might need to make a decision that means I need you gone. Away. Setting up for us when I can get there.'

She took a breath, her expression softened. 'You might be right, but what if you don't make it, I can help swing the odds in our favour.'

'I have no idea what comes next, but I know what I want after.' He put his hand over hers. She nodded and got up, walking off towards the restrooms.

Alex quickly ran a search on his cell phone for the next flights out of the country. Time was ticking, a sense of urgency had overcome him. Every single fibre of his body told him the end was near. There were three flight options within what remained of the day.

Misha returned to their booth; he could see that she had been crying. Her facial expression told him 'I'm fine'. He decided not to probe and get straight to the point. 'There are three flights out the country today.' He palmed at his beard. 'Acapulco, Buenos Aires or San Jose, Costa Rica. I need to you pick one, get us somewhere to start out and put all this behind us. I'll end this and we can move on.'

Her eyes swept from his face to her coffee, staring into it as if had the answer for her. 'I know this is the right thing, I just wish it could be different. When?'

'You have your passport?' He asked and tossed back the last of his coffee. Misha nodded. 'Then I'll drop you at the airport before I go back for Truman.'

'Fuck, I feel sick thinking about this.' Misha decided the subtle approach inadequate. Alex flashed a sympathetic smile and got up out of the booth. Misha followed. He left a few bills on the table and they left.

Misha fumbled about with her holdall, removing any contraband, ammunition, a knife, and she checked the amount of cash a traveller can legally carry when leaving the United States on her cell phone. Alex spoke. 'I'm sure its ten grand or under without having to fill out the forms. Don't worry I've already sent you enough on the wire.' She nodded as he spoke, focusing on her task. 'You need to decide the destination, there were plenty tickets to each when I checked.'

'How will you know?' She looked at him, a touch of disappointment on her face.

'Send me a text. Co-ordinates only. I'll find you when I am free of all this.' He looked between the road and her as he drove. 'The text needs to be from a cell you buy when you get there, a burner.' He could see the emotion bubbling away under her exterior. 'There is no other way, Misha.'

The journey to the international airport took most of the hour, Misha wished it was longer, she also wished there was, in fact, another option. She trusted Alex, she knew he had good inside him, but she also knew there was zero chance he would stop until The Arc of Evermore were a headline in an old newspaper, something that used to be a thing, a footnote in history.

As Alex put the vehicle into Park, his hand was barely off the stick and Misha launched herself at him, she wrapped her arms around him. He could feel the rhythmical sobbing as she tried to subdue it. A lump formed in his own throat as he realised this may be the last time, he saw her. 'It's a see you later, this is not a goodbye.' He said it conviction, truth be told, he wasn't sure himself if it was true.

'Yeah.' She sniffed, wiped a tear. 'And if it's not, I'll find you and kick your ass!' Her attempt at a laugh lasted a mere second before she started crying.

He pulled her in, kissing her, smelling the subtle sweetness of her perfume, her tense posture reminded him of her injured ribs as she guarded, wincing a little. 'You should get going, remember co-ordinates, new cell phone, okay?' He said, trying to give her some hope, some reassurance that he would be coming.

'Yeah, yeah, just don't take too long handsome.' She said, kissing him and getting out the car.

He sat watching her as she walked to the automatic doors. As they opened, she turned back, smiled and waved, the pain on her face could not be hidden by her smile. Alex smiled and waved back before she disappeared inside the terminal.

Chapter 33

Truman stood inside the awning in front of the house when Alex pulled up at the kerb. His face was cleaned up, a neat patch covered the eye that had been desecrated, his usual amber tint glasses sat resting on his nose. He wore different clothes, adding fuel to the idea that the woman and him were an item, or at least had been. His cell phone was stuck to his ear as he wore an expression of a young child being told no, for the first time. Alex looked at him as he walked down the path toward the car. He knew Truman wasn't an average man, he had some mileage from his own time in the military, black ops and whatever else he had been doing in the darkness, he acknowledged not many people would take a wire hanger in the eye and keep going not long after. He was a tough son of a bitch.

The car shook as Truman took the front passenger seat and slammed the door shut. 'Tell me you sent her away Brody.' He craned his neck around in an effort that suggested he was trying to adjust to only having one functioning eye, his good eye, was focused on Alex. 'This is fucking bad. If bad could get worse to a fucking level unheard of then this is it.'

'She gone. No longer involved.' Alex pulled away from the kerb and used a turning circle to get out of the street.

'Did that fucking psycho see her?' Truman decided to put on his seatbelt. His movements looked to be over the top. Exaggerated. Alex wondered if it was contributed to by the recent impairment or whatever drugs he had been given. 'The man wants us to go in, that's the bad news.' Truman coughed and spat something into his handkerchief. 'The fucking fucked up part is that he's at the hangar already. This is bad Brody. How bad, I don't know.'

'Did you tell him what happened? Assuming we need to go now?'

Truman pulled a .357 magnum from his coat. 'No. He knows already. That is point one on the fucking motherfucker scale. Yeah, we go, now.'

Alex hadn't anything else to say to Truman and concentrated on driving to the airfield. Truman shifted in his seat. The anxiety was enough to unsettle Alex a little. He rooted around in the rear of the car, pulling Alex's M4 into the front, running the breech and mag through his standard checks. Alex wondered hoe much his shooting would be affected by the eye.

'I have couple grenades in the trunk and my sidearm under the seat, you wanna check them also?' Alex was becoming annoyed, frustrated, feeling that Truman knew what was coming and wasn't being very transparent. 'We going to war here Ed? I need to know.'

'I don't fucking know Brody! I can't get a bead on it. It's not right, I can say that at least, Shit!' He slammed a fist onto the dash in front of him.

A new sentry populated the gatehouse at R. R Jackton. He greeted Truman with 'sir'. His face did not conceal the shock at Trumans modified appearance. Truman noticed, 'The fuck is that look for? Remember who pays you asshole!' He shouted as Alex moved the car at a crawl.

Alex continued to drive slowly toward the hangar, several vehicles were sat outside, parked like a motorcade, ready to set off. The tension inside the car consumed both men as Alex parked up. 'Bring your rifle.' Ed said as he tried and missed the door handle, twice, before finally opening the door.

They entered the hangar; it had been cleaned up from the previous visit. It smelled strongly of bleach. Marcus Hall, dressed impeccably in his tailored suit, walked out from the office, his secret service guards following. 'Ed, we have some things to discuss, have your man put that rifle away.' As the Vice President ended his sentence the distinctive figure of Carl Cooper emerged from the office behind. It was as if all breathable air had been sucked out the room as he slowly walked into the open.

In a flash Alex had dropped into a tactical stance, rifle raised, Cooper between the sights, two in the chest was Alex's intent before the booming voice of Hall filled the hangar. 'Stand down, stand down!' His hands out by his sides. Two secret service operatives lowered their weapons, seconds after raising them. 'We need to talk, stop, now!' Alex lowered his rifle, sickened at what was unfolding before him. Was Hall in bed with The Arc, he wondered.

Hall ordered his men to wait in the car, they gave Alex a dirty look as they passed him on their way out to their vehicle.

'What the hell is this, Marcus?' Truman spoke. The panic in his voice something Alex had only saw in the presence of Hall. 'This fucking bald piece of shit...' His ranting stopped by a single change of body language in Marcus Hall.

'I have asked you both to come in, we have a resolution in hand, to end this.' Hall spoke, hands dancing through the air in typical politician fashion.

Alex's eyes never left Cooper as he stood wearing a disgusting smirk on his face. His nose, or what was left of it existed below an odd white dressing that was secured with surgical tape across his cheekbones. Truman finally raged. 'Are you fucking kidding me, that noseless bastard took my eye! Yet here you are, my fucking friend of how many years Marcus, standing on his side? Is that it? Have you taken a side now?' Truman's face red, particles of spit flying out his mouth as he shouted. Alex did not see that twist coming, he thought Truman was so far under Hall's thumb to ever challenge him like this.

'Ed, this is business, calm yourself down.' Hall and Cooper walked closer. The four men were now arranged in a standoff. 'You and the Nothingman here, will stand down, an agreement has been reached.' The sheer audacity of Marcus Hall made Alex's blood boil; he knew if he had to drop the Vice President he would have no reservations. How could he possibly think Alex would stop now.

Cooper lifted his right hand to his mouth. Alex could hear the click of a mic before Cooper whispered something into it. He had comms.

Truman started again, 'Marcus what the fuck have you done?'

'Enoch will step down from office.' He swept his hand in an arc pointing out both Truman and Alex. 'You two cease and desist, let these people go about their business.'

Alex could feel his blood boiling. The pulsing of the arteries inside him delivering oxygen rich blood, readying him for any situation. He held the M4 in one hand, he would back himself to shoot Cooper first, then Marcus Hall, he knew that could mean Truman would be the last to fall. His grip intensified. He heard a vehicle door closing beyond the door of the hangar. Cooper slowly walked around until he was neither standing onside with the Vice President or Alex and Truman.

'Where is the woman?' Cooper asked, a smarmy look upon his disfigured face. 'She owes me, blood or a sorry, those men meant something to me.'

Alex's eyes bored a hole through him. 'Off limits.'

'Mmm hmmm.' Cooper smiled, his snake like appearance made Alex's skin crawl. 'She killed two of my men, that does not go unanswered.'

'Fuck you, the fact you are still alive is fucking going against every fibre in my being!' Truman shouted. Rage seething through him.

Alex picked up the footsteps before the door opened behind him and Truman. Terrence Enoch walked in, dressed as a senator should, a large pot belly testing the buttons of his shirt, a thick double chin concealed the knot of his tie as it hung over his collar. Thinned out slick back hair, the colour coming from a bottle no doubt. He stopped alongside his attack dog, Cooper. 'Well, I'm glad we can all meet up right here, sort this little thing right out.' A thick Kentucky accent cut the silence. 'Which one a you they call the Nothingman?' His gaze cast over Truman and Alex, then back to Alex. 'Well son, no need to answer that I know now, I see it in the eyes. You have caused me some inconveniences lately boy.' He flashed his over-white teeth, likely bought and claimed on back taxes to maintain his public image. 'Marcus have your puppy dog drop his gun or I close negotiations.'

Marcus Hall let the room know something wasn't right, his face spoke before his voice did. 'Negotiations? The deal was set, done, that is why we are here Enoch!'

'I will not respond to threats, he is threatening, standing there like a fucking crazy person.' Enoch snarled.

Alex ran his eyes over all that stood in the hangar. Truman looked angry and confused. Was it possible he wasn't in on whatever this was? Marcus Hall looked as angry as he was when he tore into Truman in their previous meeting, his brow reflecting the light from the beads of sweat forming. Could it be that he was now being played, terms and conditions reneged? Cooper stood, his eyes twitching over Truman and Alex. Enoch had the look of a man that knows all your secrets and has the upper hand, a dangerous position to try and hold, being wrong could be the very end for the man who thinks he is the smartest.

Alex tossed the M4 on to a crate that sat off to the side of where they stood. He saw Enoch's eyes dart to the pistol holstered to his leg and he unsnapped the strap, throwing it away also.

'Good. This is progress gentlemen.' Enoch's double chin jiggled as he spoke, it irritated Alex.

'Let's cut the shit Enoch, what the fuck kind of game are you playing here?' Marcus held his hands out, palms toward Enoch. That was his first mistake, a passive, non-threatening approach was not what worked with these people.

'I step down, you can have your uncontested run for the big seat.' Enoch looked at Cooper before speaking again. 'You stop your clandestine campaign against my organisation, but.' A dramatic pause, Alex seen it coming, this man was weak, he was used to having the scared and vulnerable around him. 'The Nothingman and Ed Fucking Truman here, who my friend here has unfinished business with, are handed over to us.'

'And the woman!' Cooper added.

Truman shuffled where he stood, laughing, making gestures with his hands, mumbling words as if he was trying to rationalise what had just been said. It unsettled Cooper who had reached into the small of his back and stopped when it looked as though Truman was having a mental break down.

'Nothingman, I will put a bullet in you myself, but your friend, well he will be at the mercy of Mr Cooper here.'

'Wait a fucking minute here!' Marcus Hall snapped. 'The deal was done, you know how to do business Terrence, this is not the way!'

'You have two minutes to provide me with your answer Marcus. Your security team are laying dead in your car. If you decline, everyone dies, these two bastards, your family, and you.' Enoch's face reddening as he spoke.

'Ed.' Marcus Hall spoke. 'I really am sorry, but you know how far I will go to get to where I want.'

'Fuck you! You are going to wish you were dead if this piece of shit fails to finish me, I swear to fucking God Marcus!' Truman spat his venom filled words at Marcus Hall.

'Okay, deal done, Mr Cooper, hand me your gun.' Enoch held his left hand out.

Cooper placed a Sig-Sauer 9mm into the hand of Enoch. He had barely taken grasp of it when he squeezed the trigger. The shot hit Marcus Hall in the upper right-hand side of his chest, nearer the shoulder, away from any vital organs, the large man stumbled backward before hitting the ground. His moan was interrupted by the voice of Enoch. 'It needs to look legitimate Marcus, these two killed your men, you, the American hero, killed them after they shot you.' He laughed as he swung his arm round to where Alex and Truman stood.

Alex heard the large inhalation from Truman, he knew he wasn't going down without a fight, Truman reached behind himself with a speed unexpected from the stocky, one-eyed man that looked as if he had lost his mind just a few moments ago. Alex bolted toward Enoch and Cooper as he heard the booming sound come from the .357 magnum Truman had just discharged. A large red cloud sprayed from the back of Enoch's head as bone and brain sailed through the air. Cooper had flinched at the shot, and it was enough of a window for Alex to get close enough to launch an attack with his fists. Thud after thud echoed in the hangar as Alex pummelled Coopers face. Cooper had fallen backwards taking Alex with him. The momentum, forced his head off the concrete, bouncing. Alex delivered several heavy elbows to the side of Cooper's head before he heard Truman screaming at him. 'Stop!'

Truman placed a hand on Alex's shoulder, grounding him, before he killed Cooper. Alex got up and looked around the room. Terrence Enoch lay nearby with only half of his head remaining. Marcus Hall had dragged himself along the floor and was sat watching, a large hand putting pressure on the bullet wound.

Truman looked down at Cooper as he lay bleeding, a bloody smile on his face. 'I think you are unlucky Cooper; this would be nicer for you if I had a fucking wire coat hanger!' Truman pushed his glasses up his nose and launched himself down on to Cooper and pressed both his thumbs into his eye sockets. The blood curdling screams of Cooper lasted for at least a minute. The limb twitching and shaking took a little longer. Truman breathed heavily as he increased the pressure, literally squeezing the life from Carl Cooper. Truman smashed the dead man's skull against the concrete for good measure before he was satisfied.

Truman got up to his feet. His thumbs were saturated in blood from the tip to where they met the hand itself. 'He will have had someone waiting outside, think you can get em in here?'

Alex nodded, he walked to the door and looked outside. A man stood against the bumper of a vehicle. Alex waved him inside. 'We're done.' The man walked through the doorway and Alex grabbed him in a chokehold, kicking at his heels forcing him forward.

'Let him go.' Truman said. Alex pushed the man toward his boss, he stumbled before Truman shot a massive hole in his chest with his .357.

'Ed, good job.' Marcus Hall coughed as he spoke. 'Now, get me into a car and to a hospital.'

'No.' Truman pulled his handkerchief from his pocket. 'You as good as fed us to them. What the fuck is wrong with you?'

'It was a bluff Ed, come on, don't be so precious.' Marcus Hall sweated profusely, he looked a poor excuse for the all-American footballer, President in waiting.

'What happened here Marcus, was you let your greed cloud what is right and what is wrong.' Truman picked up the gun Enoch had dropped, the handkerchief between his hand and the metal. 'Brody would have done what he intended, he could not be stopped, you cannot simply switch that off.' He walked closer to where Hall was sat, bleeding. 'Vice president meets cult leader to negotiate surrender and is killed in the process.' Truman swivelled, looking at Alex, and them back to Marcus Hall. 'That sounds like a good fucking headline.'

'Ed, stop playing and get me up, we can let this go and take the credit together, get you back onside after those experiments!' Hall held out his hand, expecting Truman to take it. 'Brody, you can go now, the United States of America appreciates your service.'

'Remember the Gulf, Marcus, all we have done together, do you remember when Karyna delivered my dead kid? Was any of that in your head when you decided to give me over to them?' Truman shouted, a level of emotion in his voice Alex had not thought possible. It was at that moment Hall looked defeated, nothing he would say could talk Truman off the edge.

Truman fired one shot into the head of Vice President Marcus Hall. He slowly fell over to the side as any tone left his body. Tuman tossed the gun over to where Enoch lay.

Alex watched, he noted that today was history in the making, a day that could never be taken back. Truman walked into his office, returning holding two glasses and a bottle of Pappy Van Winkle bourbon.

He poured them both an unregulated pour, could have been three fingers or four, it didn't matter and chinked the glasses together. 'Arc no more.' He looked down at his dead friend.

Alex savoured the bourbon and its warmth as it went down his throat. 'That's good, One for the road?' He had no idea what would come next, in his worst-case scenario he expected that only one of them would leave the hangar alive but there was look on Truman's face that told him he was wrong. Truman poured another.

'Brody, I have something for you, then we part ways.' Truman took his bourbon in one go and walked off into his office. Alex retrieved the M4 and his pistol whilst he waited for Ed to return.

Truman walked out the office, he looked at his friend lying dead on the floor as he passed him, shaking his head. He handed Alex a small pen drive. 'You need to see what's on this. It is engineered to remain encrypted for 48 hours after you plug it into a computer, then the data will be available for you to view.' Truman held out his hand. 'Give me your latest ID.' Alex handed him the driver's license that said he was Joel Gray. Truman walked over to the man he had shot in the chest and checked his pockets. Satisfied, he shoved the Joel Grey ID inside a pocket and blew the man's head off with his .357 magnum.

'To the Nothingman!' Ed Truman held up his bottle of Pappy and took a large gulp. 'Leave the rifle, it'll be on a flight to the middle east by morning, untraceable.' Alex placed it on a crate and took another drink from his bourbon. 'The good must not only understand evil, but become it to extinguish it Brody, you have stopped the innocent becoming a fuel for that evil.'

Alex nodded, he understood Trumans analogy and wished it was as easy to accept the things he had done. 'See you around.' He said as he turned and walked out the hangar.

Alex drove for an hour before he pulled over in a layby. He fished out the photo he had of Sarah and Emily, from that vacation he missed. His bag sat on the passenger seat, cash and his counterfeit passports lay on top of his clothes. He was unsure of how long he sat looking at the photo, but he cried uncontrollably, longer than he had done since he was a child. He wondered if Misha had made it, if she was safe. The sadness he had pushed down for so long consumed him. He knew this moment would come, he did not know when it would, but it was here. The tears did not stop, no amount of wiping or trying to take a deep breath helped subdue them. His pain was immeasurable, it was deep inside, a kind of pain that cannot be touched or tamed by medication.

He placed the photo of Sarah and Emily on to the dash in front of him, took a breath, and reached for his gun.

A pull at the slide chambered a round into his pistol. He looked at the gun, wondered how many men had fallen by it up until this point. Another deep breath. He placed the muzzle of his gun into his mouth, closed his eyes and pulled the trigger.

Chapter 34

The sound of the waves, lapping up onto the golden sands filled the air. Seabirds squawked as they looked for any opportunity for an easy meal from the beachgoers. The salted smell of the Ocean filled her nostrils. Her feet sinking into the sand as she walked reminded her how different life could be. Misha had already checked her new cell phone for his reply. She had texted Alex; 16.7483 degrees north, 99.7646 degrees west. It was the coordinates for Barra Vieja beach in Acapulco. She had rented a small apartment near the beach, bought herself a small handgun and a laptop computer within hours of arrival, two days earlier.

She flattened out her sundress and sat down on the sand, the warmth of the sun helped her feel slightly more relaxed, she checked that the message that left her outbox. It was in the sent folder. It must have been the twentieth time she had checked. She squinted in the sun reading the news from back home, she gasped as she read the headline story.

Vice President Marcus Hall dead at the hands of heinous cult The Arc of Evermore: Hall, 48, was shot dead as he brokered the surrender of cult leader Terrence Enoch, the shadow leader of The Arc of Evermore. Earlier this month the public face of the cult, Harvey Jupiter was apprehended and killed after murdering our very own Gina Santos. Amongst the dead were several cult members, Carl Cooper, Joel Grey and members of the Vice President's personal security team. Private military logistics co-ordinator Ed Truman refused comment on the events that unfolded at one of his distribution sites.

A feeling of nausea overcame Misha as she read the meat of the article. She felt short of breath and had to take a moment before she got up from the sand. Her thoughts were of Alex, had he been killed, had Ed Truman double crossed him, was he injured somewhere? Irrational thoughts consumed her and spilled out as she walked back along the beach to the apartment. She still had her old cell phone, she would call Truman, she would fly back and look for Alex. She decided to go back and use the laptop to read the other news articles, she may find something that told her about Alex. She needed hope, something to cling to, she didn't want to be alone, without him. She wondered if she was too selfish, if her wants, needs, were doomed from that moment in Manny's kitchen.

Chapter 35

The sand of the Barra Vieja beach was golden, it was almost flawless. He would not have seen this beautiful vista had the Glock not misfired a few days ago. He thought he deserved to die, wanted to die, but somehow, here he was. He sat on his bag as he looked out, filling his nostrils with the salty air. He thought about how much he wanted the gun to blow his brains out all over that car, but when he saw her, walking in his direction just a few hundred yards away, he knew he would rather be here. He had lost so much, yet the world kept turning, seconds still passed, he had found something that he never thought possible after Sarah and Emily.

She wore a loose thin sundress that fluttered in the ocean breeze. He could see the outline of a teal bikini through it. Her sandals, held in one hand, a cell phone in the other, she did not see him at first, her eyes flitted on the sand in front of her feet or cast out to the Pacific as she strolled.

He stood when she was around ten metres from him, she shook sand off her feet and looked up. At first the look was of disbelief, then of elation. She ran towards him, her cell phone and sandals resting in the sand as if they did not matter. He wrapped his arms around her, lifting her feet off the sand. She sobbed, kissed him and sobbed some more. He had already decided that she would never know of his moment after the hangar, with the gun. 'Hey, you, this is the later I was talking about, sorry it took so long.' Alex kissed her.

'I thought... never mind what I thought, those Ray Bans look good on you!' She laughed and broke away from him to retrieve her things from the warm sand. 'Let's go, I got us a short term on a little apartment.' She grabbed his hand as he scooped up his bag and followed. He could feel her excitement and energy coursing through her hand.

He told her everything as they walked, about Truman, Hall, Enoch and Cooper. He told her he was travelling under a different alias and the one mentioned on the news was something Truman had done. 'Do you know where I could access a computer? Ed gave me something, told me to check it. Then we can put this away, forever'

'Yeah, at the apartment, I got a laptop a few days ago, thought I'd need to start looking for work soon so bought one.' Misha smiled, taking his sunglasses off and trying them on for herself as they neared their apartment. They looked better on her, she knew it as she used the reflections in windows to confirm.

The apartment was small. One bedroom. A studio living area and kitchen, balcony and shower room adjoining the bedroom. It was all they needed for now. Misha pulled two bottles of Modelo from the cooler, passing one to Alex as he plugged in the pen drive to her laptop. The cold beer, open doors leading to the balcony, Alex smiled to himself, he could get used to this he thought. Misha smiled at him as she ate potato chips, leaning against the breakfast bar.

Alex opened the pen drive, there was four folders, numbered 1-4. Misha looked over his shoulder as he began to open them. Folder 1 contained a list of wealthy men, from the business world and the entertainment industry. A brief statement described them as elite figures of a country wide paedophile ring, men too powerful for the justice system.

Names of victims were listed alongside the acts of depravity enacted upon them. Alex felt sick as he read it.

Folder 2 contained files and satellite images of several remote areas. The files named an organisation called Apex inc. an organisation that allowed the wealthy to hunt, torture and murder the homeless, the addicted and illegal immigrants. For the right price, a person could live out their wildest fantasies of cruelty. A list of more people that the justice system failed more than it helped was attached. Alex could see a theme developing, he knew why Truman had given him this.

Folder 3 contained login details and a message from Truman. It read: If you are reading this then I know you will do the right thing. The login will take you to a forum where you will see the accounts of the innocent who need a Nothingman, people we have failed as a nation, people who are deemed insignificant by those who prey upon them. The next folder may result in you coming for me, I trust you will do the right thing. Ed.

Alex looked at Misha. Her crunching had stopped after reading the second folder. Her face was somewhere between dread and sadness.

Alex chose not to speak; he clicked on folder 4. It opened an official document trail. The first page detailed a Federal assignment. It was instructions to extract two unnamed witnesses involved in a classified operation. Areas were redacted, mostly sections that would contain dates and details of the agents assigned to the task. He scrolled on to the next page. His heart sank in his chest when he read his own name. Alex Brody, father, killed in action on overseas operations. Squad details redacted. He could feel his pulse racing. His breathing hastened; a tightness wrapped across his chest. He read on, despite every fibre of his being warning him to stop. Sarah Brody, mother, killed on locus. Witness 1, young female child, subject of relocation following domestic terror attack (33rd street) in which two civilians were pronounced dead on scene. He felt dizzy, he stood up and raced to the sink where he vomited. Misha stood with her hand over her mouth, her bottle of beer smashing as it hit the ground, spilling glass and golden liquid on the tiles.

Alex splashed his face with water and bolted back to the computer. He scrolled the rest of the document, looking for a location, names, anything that told him where she was. He was visibly shaking. The next words hurt his throat as he spoke them, as though the letters were made of razor blades, cutting as they filtered up from his larynx all the way to his mouth.

'Emily is alive.'

The End

Don't miss out!

Visit the website below and you can sign up to receive emails whenever Darren McGuinness publishes a new book. There's no charge and no obligation.

https://books2read.com/r/B-A-KGMY-YFFJC

BOOKS 2 READ

Connecting independent readers to independent writers.

About the Author

Darren began writing fiction in 2022, first publishing The Nothingman on ebook and paperback. With a writing style that is accessible and heavy on character and a scene orientated narrative he allows the reader to connect and become entwinted in the charater's perspective.

Darren draws a lot of his inspiration from his own experience growing up and working in and around Glasgow, Scotland. With a background as a Paramedic working in prehosptial emergency healthcare he describes it as a priviledge to experience humanity in it's best, worst, happiest, sad and most weird and wonderful!

Darren is always keen and engaging to hear what his readers think about his work and can be followed on social media @dmcguinnessauthor (Instagram) or emailed direct at Dmcguinnesswrites@outlook.com

Ingram Content Group UK Ltd.
Milton Keynes UK
UKHW042004200623
423745UK00004B/127

9 798223 725521